I0548173

Kingdom Far Away

A Thriller

Ekeh Joe Obinna

Base5 Publishers Ltd
No. 36 Limca Road Onitsha, Anambra State, Nigeria.

Base5 Publishers Ltd.
No.36 Limca Road , Onitsha, Anambra State, Nigeria.

ISBN: 978-35073-2X

email: machine_u@yahoo.com
(+234) 08063077041
Facebook.com: Ekeh Joe Obinna

DEDICATIONS

To God, who showed me how,
To my family, (parents)
Who showed me why,
And to friends, who showed me ways.

ACKNOWLEDGMENTS

A huge debt of thanks is owed to the following: Ceno Ventures Ltd, Mr. Agoha Bob, Queeneth, Ruth, Mrs. Patience C, KC Linda, Franok Properties Ltd, Mr. Agoha Harrison C, Franko Bookshop: Sir Jezz, Editor Mrs. Chinwendu Chukwuneke, Maduekwe Callista M800, Augustina Nwaokike Ujunwa, Base5 Publishers, Members of Co-Creators Universe, Mrs. Chinwe F. Ojukwu State Coordinator, National Youth Service Corps, Imo State Nigeria.

Finally, thank you Ekeh Joe Obinna.

ONE

That Friday afternoon, she had arranged to go for her lectures with her friend, Adanna, but found herself in a mood of uncertainty, which she had nursed for so long in her mind. Stream of thoughts flooded her mind that she could not really concentrate on any. She stood at the corridor and stared at no place in particular. The sun was very intense that afternoon. If she had gone to school and waited till afternoon, she would have been very sorry for herself. The scorching sun would not have been fair to such pretty skin like hers. She was a beautiful lady indeed.

Oluchi brought down her eyes from where she had fixed them as she tried to concentrate on a single thought. She felt her nose seedy so she used her fingers to clean her nostrils. She moved inside the bedroom immediately in a rush, stepping her feet two times in a second. She lay down in a bed and folded her two hands which were vibrating on the mattress. The sounds of her breathing could be heard from afar. She was shaking and rolling on the bed, followed by unconnected power of emotion that brought about heavy shedding of tears for few minutes.

It was not her first time. It started many years ago when twins were considered as evil; when the customs and traditions of some people determine their fate. Besides, this was the land where people worshiped one particular god or gods of their forefathers or better still went to their medicine men and begged for children.

Oluchi went on vibrating for some minutes, then the vibration stopped. Flood of hot tears strolling down her face provided serious food for thought running in her mind. Will I really survive this? She worried. She unfolded her hands, and then sat on the mattress with her back resting on the wall. Tears continued rolling down.

Really, it was not what she could physically subdue. The spirit that hypnotized her started when she was born. She was crying because

1

what was hypnotizing her was affecting her mental capability. If she had wanted anything that could save her out of it all, she wouldn't have wanted any prophet or prophetess. The spiritualist she trusted had been working, trying to disengage her from a spiritual husband and to save her from speaking to nobody while walking along the road. The story of having sex in her dream had been a recurring nightmare that it was no longer an attractive matter. Presently, she seriously could not see herself getting ready for school again. She was really wondering when she would be disconnected from the spiritual husband. Oluchi sat down speaking to nobody in particular. There was no perfect strategy for one to understand what she was speaking. These were the language of Moabites and Ammonites, the ancestors of the olden days that determined the present day.

A knock came at the door. She managed to listen carefully as she waited to hear it come again. The monster in her life was that her father slept with a river goddess before sleeping with her mother to conceive. All was in the name of seeking a child.

The knock came again and the door opened. Though she saw nobody, yet she heard footsteps coming closer to her. She was not surprised. That was not her first experience. But, there was something about the entrance that made her wondered for more seconds. Somebody was really coming. The entrance she was looking at was not really her door. The entrance was too narrow and straight, and there was nobody coming in. Yet, she could hear footsteps coming closer. She was to turn the other way round because the footsteps were coming behind her. She got to turn around now.

"Oluchi!" A voice called. Then, there were fingers on her shoulder.

"Oh my mother!" She shouted and jumped from her position.

"It's me, Ada. It's me," Adanna tried to hold her tight. She breathed heavily as she bent her head down. She tried to control herself to gain a steady breath.

"What is it? What is happening to you?" Adanna asked.

The tears on Oluchi's face got Adanna more confused. Adanna moved closer to her, held her wrist and drew her to herself. She anchored her hand on her waist to calm her down.

"Tell me, what happened?" Adanna implored.

Oluchi cleaned her eyes, opened her mouth to speak but tears didn't allow her. The matter was that she could not be alone. A spirit followed her around. If she was sleeping, her legs were put apart. If she was walking, she spoke to invisible beings. If she was eating, she shouted to unseen people. But when she was with somebody, they would all be gone. Why?

This was an engagement with the spirit of a river goddess in a river at a neighbouring village. An agony familiar to most people. The road to the river was unknown to anybody, yet people were passing. It was an isolated dirty road which cut a straight narrow swath through the little forest, from one village to another village. To everybody, the ground was cool as moist sand scattered in tiny clumps. To an untrained human ear, it was quiet, but if you were initiated, you would hear and understand every single noise.

Now, the spirit was unseen, yet powers were lifted and left in the dry hands of a great medicine man. There was a tall tree. Of course, it was a dead tall tree. Few kilometres ahead-inside; and around the centre of the village stood another similar tree. Those trees were an irregular shape, green and blotchy on the official village map, sprawling over 10,000 acres. For the most part, it was a vast unsettled expense of pines and oaks, rivers and lakes, crosshatched by forgotten trails, kept somehow unseen. Most people knew, most people avoided it, but it was a short-cut to the centre of the village, barely passable by Jeeps and motor-bikes; but people often passed in their cars because their cars had four wheels. Yet, people were passing through there.

Adanna helped her to sit on the bed. She placed a pillow at Oluchi's back to make her more comfortable. She too sat on the bed with her back on the wall.

"Wipe your tears. This is me, Adanna," she said boldly.

Oluchi fixed her eyes straight; trying to remember what she was thinking before Adanna came in. She was wondering if she could just end it all. She raised her face up and then continued.

"Many years ago," Oluchi started in tears. She hesitated, and then continued. "When I was twelve years old, my parents took me to a prophet in a neighbouring village. After stories were told, they fronted me before a tall tree. 'Your husband lives here,' they said to me." She paused and continued. "The prophet washed my head in the river and pegged my hair with sticks of local broom. He cleaned my body with white towel. After that, he told my father that I have a spiritual husband," Oluchi said with her mouth wide and her eyes nearly popping out of her head. Tears were still in her eyes.

"He took me to our house and buried a bottle of hot-drink, hair comb, sticks of local broom, red-candles tied with a black ropes, and a live lamb in our compound." She continued weeping.

"He said he would sleep with me before the spirits could leave me alone. I stayed with him for six months," Oluchi narrated in tears.

Adanna turned, looked at her and wondered if she really understood all she heard. But something told her Oluchi was not telling a mere story.

"I have a spiritual husband! I know I have a spiritual husband. He has been disturbing me." Oluchi blurted out, weeping.

Adanna was happy that Oluchi had been able to survive till now. What was happening to Oluchi was what Adanna believed, could be taken care of. She was annoyed at how Oluchi had kept quiet all the while. Adanna began to wonder if she was better than Oluchi. Sleeping with a fellow woman was no where better than having a spiritual husband. She had been a practicing lesbian for quite some

4

time. "Anyways, it is wise to seek advice," she reasoned to herself, and then turned to face Oluchi. "It's going to be all right," she said to her slowly.

Oluchi managed to drag herself out of bed, unhooked her bra, flipped it on the bed, and headed to the bathroom.

"Help me with my towel, please," she said, stretching her hand.

Adanna ogled at Oluchi whose breasts pointed out like they were immune to sagging. Oluchi was wearing colourful underwear, and Adanna ran her eyes on Oluchi's body such that if it were possible, she would have striped the underwear off Oluchi. She stood there fantasising on how it would feel to touch the spotless skin until Oluchi used her palms to cover her nakedness.

"Adanna, what is it? Please help me with my towel, will you?" Oluchi shouted and jolted Adanna out of her reverie.

"I think I like your wears. It looks nice on you," she commended with smiles.

Oluchi went inside the bathroom and closed the door. She stretched her hand to the soap dispenser and pressed it. Soap dropped on her right palm smoothly. She closed her eyes as she lathered herself.

"Here's the towel," Adanna said as she stood by the bathroom door. "Here is the towel," she repeated. Oluchi opened the door a little, stretched her left hand and said, "Let me have it." Adanna handed the towel to her.

"I will be in the sitting room," Adanna said and turned. Just then, there was a knock on the door.

"Are you expecting anybody? She asked as she turned Her two eyes rested on a large calendar on the wall above her. The dominant paper on the wall jittered pretty nervously in a growing sign of breeze.

"It might be Esther," Oluchi said and closed the door.

"Oh Esther!" As Adanna walked reluctantly to the door, she was struck by a sudden thought. 'Sleeping with fellow women is a short cut to death; yet I am weak with Esther." She wondered. She really understood the need for spiritual and emotional change of attitude, but on her day-to-day level, she was a creature of habits. If only she could do better and engage herself with Lesbian Sex Mafia, her life would be better. It was to this end that Lesbian Sex Mafia was introduced by Support and Information Group for all women that was 18year of age and above, including transsexual and intersexual women, and all female-born transgender who feel they have a connection with, and respect for the women community.

Then she opened the door and stepped aside for Esther to come in.

"What's up?" Esther greeted and grabbed Adanna by her waist.

"Nothing," Adanna answered, and gently removed Esther's hand.

"What's happening at school?" Adanna asked as the duo walked in.

"Staff meeting, loitering students, busy restaurants," Esther replied as she tried to pulled off her shoes. She was also feeling very thirsty so she flung her bag on the bed, moved to the far corner of the room where a small fridge was placed, opened it and took a bottle of water, and then down the content.

"This fridge is not a desert," she complimented and belched.

Oluchi came out from the bathroom and toweled herself down after which she spread the towel on a cloth hanger.

"What's up, Esther?" Oluchi said as she walked to her wardrobe and picked a long hibiscus red top which she wore on black jeans trousers. She put on her black beret, sprayed perfume on her body and stood before the standing mirror. She was very pleased with what she saw so she quickly threw her personal belonging into a small leopard skin hand-bag. Finally, she picked her phone and her sunglasses which were on the table.

"I would like to see my boyfriend. So you guys should lock my door," she said to Adanna and Esther.

6

Oluchi's boyfriend, Solomon Okafor, was the only person that had stayed with her even after he was told about Oluchi's spiritual husband. He was a tall, handsome, fair and broad-shouldered man. He had a very strong heart that he was never afraid even during her attacks. At such times, instead of being afraid, he would hold her tightly till she stopped shaking.

"You will get out of this problem, everybody does eventually," he would always say to her anytime she was under the attack. He had even promised to take her to a prayerful man of God. It was a fate as good as true love.

When Solomon started dating Oluchi, he never knew there would be a twist in their fate. He had met her at a cybercafé where he had gone to create an account for his National Youth Service Scheme early that year.

Meanwhile, Esther and Adanna were thankful that she had gone, leaving her bedroom for them to continue from where they had stopped the last time they met at Esther's house.

However, the discipline of their desire had remained the background of their character. Adanna moved closer to Esther while her fingers were undoing her buttons. She put her hand into her handbag and brought out a vibrator. Esther's back was against the floor so she moved her hands behind Adanna's back so that she could not move. They stayed like that for some seconds with their eyes closed.

TWO

As Solomon sat in front of his apartment with his left palm supporting his left-side cheek. He was wondering.

A generation went and another generation came, but the earth remained the same forever. The sun rose and the sun went down, and hastened to the place where it rose. The wind blew to the south, and went round to the north; round and round the wind went, and on its circuits the wind returned. All streams ran to the sea but the sea hadn't full yet; to the place where the streams flew, there they flew again.

"Life is useless. It is all useless, useless," Solomon chanted and worried. If living things did not exist, non-living things would not be destroyed. He chanted bitterly. He felt he had spent his life working and labouring, and all he had to show for it was to fell in love with a lady who had a spiritual husband. His tears did not start today, they started three months after he started dating Oluchi. He was worried that since he slept with Oluchi, he had not been able to stop sleeping with her. He could still remember that first day they slept. Oluchi had, after kissing him, looked straight in his eyes and said; "I made my offering now and I made it as sacrifice. So, I stayed around waiting for you to come back, and here you've come! How was your day?" She asked. Her bed which was covered with colourful Italian bedspread was also perfumed with myrrh, aloes and cinnamon. The transparent night gown she wore that day showed her nakedness and got Solomon's heart thumping.

"Come, let's make love all night long. We will be happy in each other's arms," she said as she gently pulled Solomon by his tie.

When Oluchi told him she had a spiritual husband, he did not deal with it at that time because Oluchi had refused to tell him the real origin of her problem. Then, he was worried about what it meant to do business with marine spirit. Who knows if she's got kids? Solomon wondered.

What he felt for Oluchi was dangerous, and had been the ruin of too many lives. Everyone who carried fire against their hearts left their clothes burnt. It was as good as sleeping with other men's wife which was a short cut to death. One could hire a prostitute but to sleep with marine spirit would cost one everything he had.

Solomon felt he was losing his senses. "What happened to the advice my father gave me and all that my mother taught me?" He reasoned.

He remembered his father once spoke to him saying, "Now my son, listen to me. Pay attention to what I'll tell you. Do not let women deceive you. Do not let them win your heart. Do not go wondering after them. They have been the ruin of many men and caused the downfall of too many men. If you let them run your heart, you are on your way to the world of the dead. They are short-cut to the downfall of every great man," his father, Mr. Benson Okafor had said some years back.

A loud knock at the door jolted Solomon out of his thoughts. As he wanted to get up from the bed, his head hit the bed frame. He hissed, lay back on his bed, and waited for the knock to come again. Just as he expected, it came again and this time louder. If anyone had told him that one day he would wake up to see a marine woman on his mattress, he would have rejected it. What bothered him most was that Oluchi had refused him the use of protections during their love makings. Condemning the innocent idea of using protection had kept his heart beating faster than normal.

He dragged himself to the door, opened it, stepped aside, and Oluchi, a tall pretty young lady strolled in, majestically. He then locked the door and followed her behind. The thought of what he could do at that particular moment as he watched her through the stairwell into the kitchen occupied his mind. That was not Oluchi's first visit to his house. The last time she visited, Solomon enjoyed the stories she shared with him which lasted till midnight, and left them feeling sleepy the following day. Solomon stepped aside and made way for Oluchi.

He felt there were few things a man must do after being introduced to the real world. It was non-governmental, it was non segmental, it was the mission, the great chambers of life episodes. It was said that a man must have a guiding God, he must have a wife, he must make- and have children, and he must die with time. If any of these had fell in place at the wrong time, or if any of these had come to being before the other in Solomon's life, he was ruined by lack of active thinking system; that was what everybody would say. But, if any of these had excelled; he muttered as he followed her to the bedroom, nodding. Just then, she turned to him and asked; "Honey, what will you eat tonight?"

"I doubt if I'm hungry, so I would rather fast," he replied. His response bothered her mind a bit, but she would rather not ask questions concerning it.

Every day, Solomon had waited anxiously for the time Oluchi would be freed from the marine world, and perhaps from the spiritual husband. As the time hadn't come, and his life couldn't return to normal without Oluchi, Solomon became very perplexed. And then he said to Oluchi, "If your axe is blunt and you don't sharpen it, you will have to work harder to use it,"

On hearing that, Oluchi felt she could no longer keep quiet. So she asked, shaking her head; "I don't comprehend. What I feel for you, the world will not understand. I love you so much; even beyond my own understanding. Your lips cover me with kisses, your love is better than wine. There is a fragrance about you; the sound of your name recalls it. No woman can help it."

He held her two hands, drew her closer to himself with his two eyes fixed on hers.

"You are dark and beautiful; dark as desert tents of cedar, yet beautiful as the curtains in a king's palace. Your skin is better than the finest gold. Please let's deal seriously with these spirits," he said. His eyes were misty and his voice were shaky. He was already in tears.

Oluchi watched, her mouth agape in surprise. So when she spoke, she did that, slowly.

"Tell me my love, where will you lead your flock to graze?"

By then, only a thin line stood between Solomon and Oluchi. Oluchi wouldn't want this topic to bring ripples, noise, and distractions. That discussion should not continue. But there was a burden in her heart. And the burden activated profuse tears which flowed down freely from her face, down to her jaw. As soon as Solomon saw the tears, he was forced to retreat his emotions. So he held her hand and said; " God who made you is still alive. He would never make you marry a spiritual husband. Why should we need to look for Him among the flocks of the other shepherds? Isn't He here with us?" He asked in awed tones. An appalled silence followed. The noises between two of them were reduced to sobs and sniffs. He didn't want to believe that Oluchi wasn't having any cure. Maybe, no one had given her better advice and support until he came. Solomon felt incapacitated because he was not a physician, so there was nothing much he could do to help her.

"My worries will soon be over. It won't be long and everything will become right once again. I'm sure of that. I'm very sure of that," Oluchi said assuredly.

"Calm down my dear. Calm down," Solomon said comforting her.

As they came closer to each other, the television in the sitting room switched on. The light bulb which suspended from the roof switched on too. Its reflect went as far as the stairwell. Solomon stared open-eyed with terror at the bright light reflection. He was lost in thought as he wondered what was happening. But Oluchi didn't flinch at the unfolding event. She understood the rule. She knew that the law of spirit was spiritual. She considered that what they were suffering at that time would not be compared to the glory that was going to be revealed to them. All she needed was to wait with eager longing to God to retrieve her spirit-being. Not of its own will, because God did not fake hope. She felt that one day she would be freed from slavery so she could share the glorious freedom of womanhood. Few minutes thereafter, the television became mute and the light bulb went off.

"Show yourself," Solomon wanted to scream, but he couldn't. And he didn't know why. In a twinkling of an eye, the violently threatening shadow disappeared, and a soft wind from the South blew in through the window. Solomon felt it was time they went to bed.

"Let's go to bed," he said.

"One day, we would definitely bid farewell to all these," Oluchi said.

Solomon began to say his night prayer. After a long time, he was still awake as sleep had deserted him. He looked at Oluchi who was quiet and presumed that she was asleep so he sat up from the bed with his back against the wall.

"How much longer will you forget her oh Lord? Forever? How much longer will you hide your face from us? How long must she endure all this trouble? How long will sorrow fill her heart days and nights? How long will our enemies triumph over us? Look at me, oh Lord-my God, and answer me. Restore my Oluchi; don't let her die of this trouble," Solomon prayed earnestly with a broken heart and eyes filled with tears

Oluchi was touched by those words so she turned to face Solomon.

"Solo my love," she fondly called, "I will sing praises to God because He has been so good to me."

When Solomon heard that, he threw himself on the ground and continued praying. He wouldn't consider it a small matter that what

Oluchi was suffering from could ruin his plans with her. He had tried to train himself not to think about his rejections, but it still did hurt.

Oluchi gripped one of the pillows as Solomon opened his eyes, and held her. With a lot of sinking feelings, she held him unto him too. They stayed like that for minutes. Solomon tried to raise his hand but Oluchi stopped him.

"Please don't. Only if we care enough for the living, never will people die," she whispered to him.

A cold hand seemed to clutch at Oluchi's heart. If it was fear, or if it was her imagination, she couldn't say. The conflicting emotions were consuming her. Solomon's soothing hands would undoubtedly attract sleep. She wished he was never going to remove those hands circled around her. Her tightly closed eyes made her look like someone who had been sleeping for hours even though, she had been awake. She had her reasons for reacting coldly towards every event. She knew what they said would happen to her if she made a slip or if she couldn't finish fighting after she had started.

"I want us to talk about this. Did you tell your friends about this?" Solomon asked. Oluchi turned away her face. She couldn't tell him a word about the manner in which Adanna and Esther had known of it. Few people knew, but nobody was going to know of it again. Everybody thought she had a fling with demons and that was the way she would be forever.

"Esther and Adanna are my friends. I asked Esther to help me tell her father. I thought he could somehow help me out, being a Reverend Pastor," she explained.

Solomon relaxed. He doubted if Oluchi knew Adanna the way he knew her.

"Adanna is a lesbian," Solomon announced.

Oluchi hesitated. Then she said; "Yes, I was going to tell you about that. But, I was afraid you may assume that I was into that too and sever our relationship. Really, it had been on my mind to tell you. I didn't even know you were aware."

The friends Solomon knew, he was not even too sure about them. Anybody could claim to be anybody's friend until there was problem. But did that mean that nobody had gotten enough chance to proclaim his or her help to support Oluchi before this eleventh hour? How saddening it was, that after living this hard life with tumultuous years in school, that everything would be reduced to misery all in the name of spiritual husband?

Oluchi told Solomon lesbianism was a spiritual problem. It was a fate as good as having a spiritual husband. She explained to him that the thin line of difference was that spiritual husband was invisible while spirit of lesbianism dealt with fellow women. Both participants were condemned to spiritual attacks; and that, there was no redemption for both participants when the rash of time would manifest.

Oluchi and Solomon buried themselves in deep stories and thoughts. Now, Solomon had been told that Adanna's spirit was also held hostage by an evil spirit and the hypocritical nature in the heart of man had prevented her from seeking deliverance, at least for a while.

"We need to make a decision about this now," Solomon said . Oluchi lowered her gaze to the floor and raised it again. Her thoughts turned to what was said. She knew what was said. There was something Solomon had not heard about her and he needed to be told about it.

"The first movement I made in my quest for solution brought me trouble," she spoke in a low tone. It was so obvious she was tired.

Solomon stood up from the bed, placed his right hand at the nape of his neck, stretched, and yawned. Something he always did when confronted with a difficult situation that needed a difficult decision. Oluchi was about to speak but Solomon interrupted her.

"We shall fight it,"he said firmly.

Apart from the fact that Solomon was viewing the landscape through the window of his small room which was at the edge of the street. His whole thought was on how to handle Oluchi's problem. But he needed to get to the root of it all. Maybe Oluchi parents were afraid to dig too deeply, Solomon reasoned. At that moment, a plan on the way out of the problem came to his mind. He was thinking of how to go about it when Oluchi began to speak.

"Something was told," She said. There was a look of seriousness on her face.

"What was it that was told? By whom ? To whom?" Solomon asked in quick succession. An awed silence followed immediately. Oluchi closed her eyes in deep thought. She must tell Solomon nothing but the whole truth. The phone on the table rang, Oluchi stretched her hand and grabbed the phone.

"We kept your key under the door mat," the caller said as soon as Oluchi picked the call.

She knew that mellifluous voice at the other end. It was Esther's.

"Okay!" She said and ended the call. Then she heaved a sigh and continued, "Two people had tried to disentangle me from this trouble. Today, both of them are gone. I mean, they are dead," she stressed.

Solomon did not panic. He had heard a similar story before. He got up and leaned against the wall.

"Tell me the story," he said with bated breath.

"My father was a counselor. His name was Christopher Egwuatu, the former kingmaker in Umualamaeze village- my village. He got himself involved into this mess because of his quest, rather, his desire to have his own child.

She paused for breath and then continued.

"Few years ago, I was living with a man I thought was my father. But, I later got to know he wasn't. My father died when I was six as I was later informed. He died fighting for my cause. After his death, my mother got married to another man who also died fighting to separate me from a prophet I had lived with for some months. My mother got mad when I was about thirteen years old. These problems came because I was born into the world as a result of an intercession of a medicine man who serves a river goddess somewhere in neighbouring village before my village. The medicine man lives in a tree called Bumu Iroko at the heart of our village near the market square."

Solomon stared fixedly at her. He did not panic but he could feel some sweats on his neck. Deaf to subtle noise generated on either side, he heard only his breathing which was steady.

"The man I called a prophet was the medicine man," she said and yawned.

"Is that all?" Solomon queried, looking unperturbed.

A week ago, something eerie happened. Oluchi was approached by a prophet who told her that the high heeled shoe she wore was not too good for her condition. That same day, another prophet met Solomon at a fast food joint and told him that the flat footwear he wore was not meant for short people like him. Yet, Solomon wasn't short.

"He was not a prophet. He must not be a prophet," he had told himself. None of them said what happened to them that day to each other.

The cool breeze of late night hindered Solomon from making any further speculation. One thing was sure. The conversation should be suspended. It was getting very late.

"Close your eyes and sleep, it's late already,"he said quietly to her. He felt an overwhelming urge for her but he resisted the urge. He felt great pity for her. Besides, a woman with a problem of such magnitude might lose sensation, he reasoned. If she wasn't in his life, then life for him would've been a bigger illusion beyond his imagination. He never had been the kind of man that would always complained. But it was getting bigger now. Mr. Solomon, you need to settle down, he told himself.

Solomon stretched across the table for the golden cigarette case and the golden lighter. A quick glance at his wrist watch indicated that it was 14 minutes past 12 midnight. He lit the cigarette and forced the smoke to went out in a straight form.

"Who will help me fight this?" Solomon asked himself.

Something that kept him awake and made him smoke at such an unholy hour was a real trouble. He dropped the cigarette on a ceramic flat plate on the table. After fumbling with the lighter for some seconds, he drooped it too on the same plate. He really got to sleep. He knew it wouldn't be easy for him to get a good sleep considering his troubled mind but he would try anyhow. He looked at Oluchi and admired her. Listening to her snores, he could tell that she was deeply asleep.

"Who will help me fight this?" Solomon worried himself again before he finally closed his eyes.

THREE

When you get shocks that squeeze your heart beats, paralyze your brain and turn your body cold, you begin to die slowly. When Solomon woke up from sleep and remembered that the fight had just begun, a part of him left him. He reassessed his plans to ensure he hadn't taken the wrong step. He dropped his hand phone and took a glass of water.

Meanwhile, Oluchi had finished preparing their breakfast and was getting ready for her early morning lectures. One striking thing about her was that she had taken falling in love seriously so she always made sure Solomon had something to eat any time she was around.

"Who will help me fight this?" A question that had been on his mind for a long time. Solomon's heartbeat was beating very fast. Although the cool morning breeze was seeping into the bedroom through the window, and yet, Solomon's brow was covered with sweat. On getting out from the bathroom, Oluchi was dazed to see Solomon sweating. She knew he wasn't sweating because of fear but for the zeal to get her freed. So she behaved as if she didn't notice and began to dress up.

For Solomon, everything had changed and was never going to be the same again. But it was all-a crazy thing to Solomon. There was no difference. Every day was just the same thing. It had been months since he met Oluchi. He just wanted to know if anybody out there was feeling for him. Or should he leave this trouble and go for the best of life? He felt he could not stand this raging storm alone. It was hitting down his window-proof and would soon drive him insane. The thought of the raging storm that was threatening to drown him got him really worried, and he felt his courage slipping away. He stood up from the bed and faced the standing mirror that was fixed on the wall. The image he saw in the mirror sent shivers down his spine.

Oluchi was no longer comfortable with the wall of silence so she had to break it. She waved her right hand across his face to draw his attention. Then she asked;

"Where have you been?"

"Too many thoughts on my mind. I can't really say which one is bothering me most. But don't worry. Go for your lectures. I will be all right," Solomon said and sat down on the bed.

"Are you sure?"

"Of course. I'm sure."

"Well, if you say so. I'm off to school. Your breakfast is in the kitchen," Oluchi said and took to the next door by her left.

* * * *　　* * * *

At nine past the hour of nine, it was becoming really sunny outside. But the white window curtains was preventing the sun from casting its rays in the bedroom. A clock above the window ticked nonstop. Solomon moved to the window. A yellow Nissan Sunny taxi pulled over by the right side of the road and a man came out from its back door. The man crossed over to the opposite walkway. He was Emmanuel Ibe, Solomon's friend. As he walked, he cast quick short glances at his wristwatch. The building had two identical stairwells that led to a particular stairway, then to upstairs. It was about fourteen footsteps onto another level. No windows. Green-painted concrete floor and cinder-block walls. A door that was made of solid wood presented itself at the edge of the stairwell. So Emmanuel moved straight. Then he stood in front of the door and knocked at the door. Immediately, Solomon opened the door. Emmanuel knew he had been watching him all along through the bedroom windows.

He was looking very refreshed as he had spent two weeks out of town going to parties. He was elated when he stumbled on a book editor at one of the parties. It had been his desire to meet an editor who will work on his novel.

"What's up man?" Emmanuel greeted him, smiling.

"Come inside. I'm all right." Solomon said. But his countenance betrayed him.

"There is something I cannot secure from another person except you," Solomon said as soon as Emmanuel sat down in one of the cream coloured leather cushion in the sitting room. Emmanuel looked at him and shoot his head. Then he got up , went over to the TV and switched it on. Solomon handed a very chilled can of Stout beer to him as he sat down

"Thanks," Emmanuel said, opened the can and gulped a half of the content. Then, he relaxed into the cushion as he dropped the can on a side stool and turned to where Solomon was sitting.

"What's that?"Emmanuel asked, his eyes was fixed on the television.

"I have spiritual troubles," Solomon said in a very low tone.

"SPIRITUAL?" Emmanuel stressed, his eyes widely opened.

* * *　　* * *

It was twenty-seven past the hour of ten when Solomon emerged from the bathroom. He spent few minutes putting on his clothes; then, after dressing his hair with a small comb, he rejoined Emmanuel in the sitting-room again.

"The only thing that doesn't make sense about life is, due to principalities, we all suffer great pains and die. But, no one offers to get in the bed with us when we die. It doesn't make sense going to heaven alone. We shouldn't leave our love ones behind."

"What troubles are you talking about?" Emmanuel asked facing him.

"I need a protection programmer."

"Physical or spiritual?"

"Anyone you can trust."

"I don't understand," he said to Solomon.

20

"It's all about Benammi and Moab, the ancestors of the present day. Do you remember Moabites and Ammonites?"

Emmanuel did not comprehend yet he nodded his head as if he did. The only deposit spirit in him was for fearlessness. He thought they would be dealing with charms and spiritual concoctions for luck and protection. While still on the thought, he remembered something that had happened to him, and said, "I have been to a church where the man of God called peoples' names and their phone numbers and made them believe that prophecies were for them. You see most pastors, prophets, and prophetesses, they are not of the Lord."

Solomon looked at him and was convinced that Emmanuel did not really understand him. He wished he could be calm but he couldn't. He lit a cigarette in order to calm his nerves.

"My man, you really don't understand. I want us to kidnap a medicine man and keep him out from his shrine for four days," Solomon said calmly, puffing his cigarette.

Emmanuel was shocked at what he heard. He wondered what it took Solomon to come up with such bizarre thoughts. "Kidnapping is a grave crime. Kidnapping a medicine man is a suicide mission." Emmanuel worried.

Moments of silence followed as their eyes rolled over and over again.

"Why would you want to do a thing like that?" Emmanuel asked, breaking the silence.

Solomon knew he needed to convince him but he would not want to press him too hard. He looked at his wristwatch and began to tap on the chair's arm. He wasn't willing to tell him everything. So he had to censor the whole story.

"Months before my girlfriend, Oluchi, was born, it was told that her parents went to a medicine man to beg for a child. There, her father was compelled to sleep with the goddess of a river near their village for three days. What I'm trying to tell you is that Oluchi originated from marine manipulations. She was dedicated to the river goddess and got married to a medicine man. The medicine man is the first male child of the river goddess." Solomon paused and looked at his friend's face. He continued as his friend's face was expressionless.

"Few months ago, I hired a bedroom in a small city called Anioma which was very close to Umualamaeze, my girlfriend's village. I studied the movement of people in the village to be accustomed to their customs and traditions. I was told that the people worship a tree in the centre of their village, around their market square. The tree is called Bumu Iroko. That was what I was told. Later, a prophet took Oluchi to his house and slept with her for few months. The old man said the prophet did it to fulfill his charms and powers of prayers because his powers are from the river goddess. The medicine man is whom I want us to kidnap," Solomon said, finally.

"I'm scared," Emmanuel who had kept quiet all the while Solomon was talking said. "I' m greatly afraid that the result might not be as good as expected," He said, shaking his head.

"All we need to do is to follow the advice of a counsellor, programmer," Solomon said and wished that Emmanuel could say something, it could anything.

"I can't do it," Emmanuel said. Solomon gave him a steady gaze which made him very uncomfortable.

All right, I will do the programming, he said.

"Programming? That's okay. But that's not the real trouble right now. If I can't secure you to partner with me, who will help me do the job? I need two partners and you're the only person I think I can tell to help me out right now. You have to understand me. This is strictly confidential and I can't go anywhere unless you're by my side," Solomon added.

"This is what we do for each other. I'll neither advise you to fight a medicine man nor help you to fight him," Emmanuel said.

"I'm not fighting a medicine man. All I want us to do is to keep him out of his shrine for three or four days to enable my fiancee to face spiritual deliverance. If I don't, she will die the day she'll say 'I do' at the altar."

"The fight of a medicine man is a fight against principalities and powers. It's not a fight of flesh and blood," Emmanuel reminded.

"Support me to keep this man out of his shrine. I have a picture of what I want to do in mind. It won't hurt anybody. We'll take him while he's asleep."

"The best I can offer you is to tell you right now that this is not going to work out the way you may have planned it. If you need a third party, it must be Oluchi; she knows the ways of the spirits," Emmanuel said.

Solomon's eyes retreated. He managed to reason through what his friend had said. He knew Oluchi could help but he didn't know how exactly. Was she going to stay with the medicine man to feed him after he had been kidnapped? No! The last thing he wished was to let the medicine man set his eyes on her. It could go a long way to destroy everything. If anything had happened that he died and had to live in a kingdom far away, Solomon would call it a fine prize. But it was certain that Oluchi had an assignment to bring him on board. Solomon proceeded on course with the belief that he did not fall in love to start fearing marine spirit or any native spirit. He believed that Almighty God, the creator of sun and moon, would protect him from any serpent venom. .

The sound of a ringing phone which was in the bedroom startled the two friends and they looked at each other apprehensively.

Emmanuel was greatly afraid and Solomon too. None of them uttered a word. The phone rang again and Solomon went for it. On realising whom the caller was, he picked the call.

"Hello baby!" He said trying to take control of his voice.

"Hello." Oluchi said.

Solomon sensed tension and uneasiness from her voice.

"Dear, is everything all right, you sound so unhappy?" Solomon asked.

"It's Esther. She had an accident. There was nothing I and Adanna could do."

"An accident! How? Where did it happen? I mean where are you now?" Solomon asked in quick succession.

"A small Toyota Camry had brake failure and ran into a small shop at New American Quarters few minutes ago. We called an ambulance which took them to New Leeds Infirmary."

"Them,...who're them?"

"Esther and the Camry driver. Please dear, I need you to come over."

"You mean now?"

"Yes, of course. Adanna and I can't really do much. I need you now please."

"Where is the Camry driver right now?" Solomon asked.

"The driver died on the spot."

"And Esther?"

There was an unappealing silence at the other end of the phone call.

"Dear, Hello. Dear, can you hear me?"

"Please come over," Oluchi said weakly and the line went dead.

Solomon's hand was shaking so he clutched tightly to the phone. He wiped the beads of sweat from his face. He looked at Emmanuel to find some succor but all he could see was fear boldly written all over face. So he moved quietly into his bedroom to get his car keys. His bedroom was spacious and his confused state of mind made it difficult for him to locate his keys which always hung on a nail by the wardrobe side. He looked so different now; something that always happened to a troubled man.

"Let's go to New Leeds Infirmary," he said to Emmanuel.

"Are you all right ?"Emmanuel asked him.

Solomon turned. "I'm all right."

"Maybe that was a wrong question. The right question should have been; what's happening at New Leeds Infirmary?"

Solomon cleared his voice.

"You're right. But when we get there, we'll help ourselves with the answer," he said slowly. Solomon had trained himself not to allow troubles affect his countenance.

They got to the hospital fifty minutes later and went straight to the emergency department. The transformation into that particular department of the hospital was something they found very unappealing. As Solomon leaned forward looking at Oluchi who was sitting on the floor, he couldn't organize the abstract concept of his train of thoughts. Something so different to Emmanuel and yet, so familiar to Solomon.

"Get up, dear," Solomon said and gently pulled Oluchi to himself and an unanticipated kiss materialized. It was as light as a butterfly's wing and Oluchi was soothed by the feeling. Far from feeling scared of what happened, she concentrated on what could happen next.

"Where are Esther and Adanna?" Solomon asked softly and Oluchi freed herself from him. If only she could trust herself enough; she could say it without passing feelings and fear.

"Esther did not survive the accident. Adanna is in the doctor's office," Oluchi answered, shaking her head and trying to fight back tears. Solomon noticed her state of mind and drew her to himself again. The doctor's door opened and Adanna staggered out. She went over to where Emmanuel was with tears streaming down her face. She looked at Emmanuel's face and said; "Esther is dead! My own Esther is dead!" Then she burst into tears.

"It's all right," Emmanuel consoled. He too never imagined Esther dead, but what could he do? He was sure that Adanna had feelings like every other girl would do, but it hurts for sure. Losing a pretty real friend hurts. If only he could trust himself to manage his tension, he was sure he could be more romantically useful to her. But, changing her character would worth more than what he thought he could emotionally subdue.

"Sit down here," Emmanuel said and pulled her away almost immediately. Solomon held unto Oluchi till the doctor came out. The doctor who had a phone in his hand turned to Solomon and said; "It's Mr. Desmond."

"I'll have it," Oluchi said as she stretched her hand to reach for the phone. As she collected the phone from the doctor, she moved away from others to answer the call. After a discussion that lasted for about eleven minutes, she rejoined others.

"It's Esther's father," she said .

"The hospital will attend to their corpses and deposit them to the mortuary," the doctor said, and they followed him to his office.

Oluchi was happy that Mr. Desmond called. At least the doctor would prepare the bill for him and her friend's corpse would be treated accordingly. Few minutes later, they were heading towards Solomon's house. None of them uttered a word all through the ride. They were greatly sad concerning Esther's sudden demise.

* * *   * * *

The wall clock on the right side of the wall of the sitting room struck 5:45pm when they got home. Solomon went straight to his bedroom with Oluchi while Adanna who was still crying because of her relationship with Esther, sat on one of the chairs in the sitting room. Emmanuel wanted to join her on that chair because he wanted to calm her down but was uncertain how she would react considering the fact that she did not fancy the opposite sex. Adanna did not behave as if someone was sitting by her side. The first time Emmanuel went closer to her she displayed no affection. Emmanuel knew that if anyone touched tar, it would stick to his hand. He felt it was better he stayed back on his seat rather than bite more than he could chew.

Solomon came out from his bedroom.

"Can I see you?" he said to Emmanuel.

Emmanuel stood up and followed him to the corridor with his two hands buried in his trouser's pockets.

"How do we do it?" Solomon asked Emmanuel. He had a serious look on his face.

"What?" Emmanuel asked, looking bewildered.

"The protection programming thing. I want it as soon as possible," Solomon said.

Emmanuel kept quiet for some time thinking on how best to approach the issue. He wondered why Solomon considered him worthy and chose him to work with him even though he had, in the past, slept with Solomon's former girlfriend, Victoria. He still remembered how Victoria spoke evil of him and insulted him despite the fact that she was the one who lured him into the act. Solomon had forgiven him when he saw how remorseful and ashamed he was concerning his actions. Then and there he made up his mind to help his friend in any way he could.

"I know of a physical programmer in Zik's Avenue," Emmanuel said, then he went on. "His name is Peter Ukachukwu. He was convicted for kidnaping in 2005, and released on parole in 2009. In

2010, he was suspected, and consequently arrested in connection with kidnaping a political godfather, Barrister Benson Ojukwu. He was released after four months in police cell- not guilty."

Solomon was dumfounded. 'So there is hope for me', he reasoned within himself. His little glimmer of hope could be enlarged if he could get this protection programmer to work for him. He neither wanted to be persistent in questions nor let his emotions control him. He had enough courage to keep him stable throughout.

"Peter will listen to you. That's why I have chosen him for you. He will tell you what to do when you meet him," Emmanuel said. He looked at his wristwatch. It was getting very late.

"So what do we do now? Solomon asked quietly.

"You've already been instructed to welcome everything he will tell us when we meet him tomorrow. You are not to argue with him. You must give complete obedience to his will. I can personally testify to you for his hard work for the people he had worked for. You must nod your head to show acceptance to everything he says. Always remember there is no room for argument. The right time to meet him tomorrow will be in the evening. That way, he will not have enough time to change his mind towards any decision made, afterwards." Solomon listened with rapt attention in order not to forget anything. He agreed with his friend that argument which was capable of destroying everything should be avoided.

"If this guy does not have the ability of using his personality to suppress mine, it would be a difficult thing because the problem is mine and I know where and how it pains me," he said passionately. Solomon's heart was thumping. He knew he needed more courage and confidence for the battle of wills with Oluchi's spiritual husband.

"But really Solomon, my dearest friend, can't you avoid this battle you are embarking on? Are you not getting too personal, too involved in this spiritual war you want to fight physically? Why don't you live your normal life? run your race the best way you could, and win eternal strength from God. Was it not this same war that consumed Oluchi's father, her foster father and made her mother mad for some years? Do you think you can win this war? Can you really fight the spirits and live to tell the story?" Emmanuel tried to talk his friend out of the perilous journey he was about to embark on.

By that time, most of the people in the neighbourhood had switched off their lights and gone to bed. The atmosphere was getting darker and cooler. It was really a breezy night. Adanna had stopped crying and was watching the television. Solomon went back to the sitting room with Emmanuel. Solomon looked at Adanna, and then, at Emmanuel who was staring at Adanna and walking closer to her.

"Good night," Solomon said to Adanna. He felt Emmanuel was going to make her more comfortable and get her to sleep well.

"Good night," She replied and smiled. Then, her attention moved back to the television again. She saw Emmanuel sitting on the next seat to hers watching the television too. Although there was no interesting programme showing on the television, Emmanuel wouldn't want to sleep while Adanna was still awake. He knew Adanna would not find things easy considering her experience with Esther who had gone with the Camry driver. Esther adored Adanna, and her demise had taken a toll on Adanna and had also given Adanna a maturity above her real age. If Adanna knew that Emmanuel was staring at her, she did not show it. So one could imagine how surprised Emmanuel was when Adanna came over to where he was sitting down and said; "May I sit with you, please?"

Emmanuel didn't utter a word, he just shifted for her. She sat down and placed her head on his laps. When Emmanuel saw that

Adanna's eyes were closed, he relaxed with his back resting on the chair, and closed his eyes.

KINGDOM FAR AWAY

Solomon thought Emmanuel would wake him up the next morning by six. But, it was 7:18am when the alarm clock on a table started beeping. He opened his eyes and looked at Oluchi who was still sleeping. Other things on the table beside the alarm clock were a pack of cigarette and a lighter. He reached for them, smiled wryly as he remembered all that he was told last night. He took out a stick of cigarette from the pack. It seemed that cigarette had been his absolute source of strength since he got to know Oluchi. That day would be his first date with Peter. After his last night's discussions with Emmanuel, he hadn't really thought things out. He knew Peter would not do those things out of the kindness of his heart. He was worried about how to face the financial arrangement with him since he did not discuss it with Emmanuel and he didn't have enough money with him. He closed his eyes. Something about his mood made him looked like a ghost. He always looked like that whenever he was battling with difficult thoughts. He moved to the toilet to ease himself. Oluchi was not woken up by smoke, but, she did wake up when the alarm clock started to beep again at 7:30. She spent few minutes in prayers and got up from the bed to do her morning exercise of press up.

Emmanuel woke up very tired. He did not sleep peacefully all through the night .He dreamt and saw himself walking on a river in a village. But he wouldn't want to think about it. If the memories could just fizzle, that would be better. He stood up and gently walked out from the room where he had slept with Adanna.

"What's this face you're putting on this morning?" Solomon

asked Emmanuel as soon as he came out from the toilet and saw Emmanuel with his two hands behind his back.

"You have to be careful,"was all Emmanuel said and ran his tongue over his dry lips after which he entered the toilet. Solomon didn't know whether the advice was for him, he just shrugged and went for his toothbrush and toothpaste.

Right there in the toilet, Emmanuel recalled what Solomon had told him during one of their afternoon drink which had become a ritual. That Oluchi was given to her parents by a river goddess. And most of the time they had dinner with Oluchi, he had wondered if he was not actually eating with the devil after casting stolen glances at her. Nevertheless, he had agreed to everything his friend-Solomon wanted even though he felt that many things concerning this issue were wrong. One of the things he felt was wrong with the whole idea was how Solomon wanted the trouble to be settled. That day was the day they had arranged to meet with the programmer but Solomon was not even ready yet. Emmanuel came out of the toilet and entered inside the bathroom.

Few minutes later, Solomon dressed in white jacket over a blue jean trousers and stood at Emmanuel's bedroom's door;

"I'm through," he said in a very low voice.

"Give me few minutes and I will join you," Emmanuel responded.

While waiting for Emmanuel, Solomon began to imagine how happy he would be after this battle has been fought and won. He was sure he would go back to his writing career. The appearance of a young man whose two hands were buried in his pockets standing beside the flower pot in the sitting room interrupted his train of thought.

"Let's go," Emmanuel said.

Solomon lugged a suitcase out from his room and Emmanuel

followed him. It took them less than ten minutes to get to the car park.

"What would you have her do? Solomon asked Emmanuel jokingly.

"Who are you talking about?"

"Adanna of course. She was with you all night," he said as he opened the car door.

"Adanna is not an opposite sex person. Lesbianism has ruined her," Emmanuel said and hissed. He was unhappy.

"The fight could be fair," Solomon said.

"What fight are you talking about?"

"Queue her out. I know you can do it. That's no fight compared to what we're fighting right now." The suggestion evoked a story inside the car. As Emmanuel was tapping his fingers on the dashboard, his mind ran through many things at once. Solomon put on his sunglasses so he could look at reflections. Then he said in a very calm voice, "That may be the one thing I ever imagined; making your life the way you want it is not a very bad idea." He smiled, and then said amusingly, "I guess it looks the way I see it. Now, put yourself in my place. Do I love what I'm doing?" He watched out traffic.

"Take your right to the next junction. That's where we'll meet him," Emmanuel explained. His voice was weak. He began to miss Adanna because Solomon had made him to realize that Adanna was not born a lesbian but she acquired it.

Solomon pulled off the road and as they approached the hotel, Emmanuel said; "Please don't banter words with him."

Something flashed through Solomon's mind as his hand phone started ringing. He reached for it.

"Why didn't you want to tell me?" The voice which indicated that the caller was crying, asked. Solomon knew that voice so he struggled to give a convincing answer.

"I was going to tell you when I'm ready," he responded. " I will meet you for lunch after school and tell you. Just take care," he said, then ended the call. The caller was Oluchi.

The duo alighted from the car and walked towards a long brick building. Then they got to a big restaurant. It was a very nice building that he would want to take Oluchi to, for lunch, that afternoon. They had walked a few metres away from the big restaurant when he remembered something about that building. That was where he met a man who called himself a prophet and told him that the flat footwear he wore the last time was not too good for short people like him. Something happened again that made him nearly hit his head on a wall if not for Emmanuel who stopped him.

"What are you looking at?" Emmanuel asked, shielding him.

"That man over there seems…." His voice tailed away as he hit his head on the wall. "Oh no!..it's painful."

"I'm sorry," Emmanuel pitied him. People who were around even noticed what happened and stared at him. Solomon shook his head. The whole lots of things had started to make meaning to him. But what? What was it telling?

Solomon and Emmanuel were directed to sit on a long framed seat in the reception room as they entered the building. They were nervous when a huge man walked up to them and asked; "Please I am looking for my wife. Do you guys see any young lady in pink gown with a white hand bag?"

The two friends exchanged looks.

"No! We just came in now on appointment," Emmanuel replied to the who turned and took a walk.

The upholstery was comfortable to sit on but not rich. The inexpensive wall clock struck 10:21am. Solomon wondered why things were getting faster and untreated than the way the schemes were arranged. Emmanuel looked up and saw a man walking up to them, "That's him," he said. "Peter," he repeated himself. They both stared at him as he came closer.

"Gentlemen, let's talk," he said and shook hands with the two friends. Solomon was expectant when Peter showed up. And the way he led them to a clump of shrubs behind the building to talk got him convinced that he was worth his onions. "Tough young guy," Solomon wondered. He was immediately impressed by his efficiency. By that time, the morning sun was coming up.

"My name is Peter Ukachukwu. I am a counselor. I anticipate that something is about to happen but needs programming. If so, I will programme a good plan. Otherwise, I'm a sick man for you guys," Peter said as soon as they were out of earshot.

The two friends both nodded. Emmanuel leaned back and placed his two fingers on his lips. Solomon relaxed on his position too.

"I guess we have a business to look into," Solomon said to Peter.

"Print it out," Peter said.

Solomon quietly brought out a piece of paper from his pocket. He looked at the paper and jolted up again.

"My fiancee is under the attack of a medicine man. She was spiritually dedicated to a river goddess and got married to the medicine man. I want us to keep the medicine man out of his shrine for three to four days to enable my fiancée to face spiritual deliverance by a true man of God." Solomon narrated while Emmanuel nodded his head in support.

When Peter heard that, his eyes widened like those of Egyptian statues. Peter had known that he was wanted to kidnap a medicine man, but, he did not panic. He seemed so fearless; and that gave more hope to the two friends. Peter looked at Solomon speaking, not with amazement, but with curiosity. Was Solomon all that unfeeling? He didn't think so. He saw the sickly smile on

34

Emmanuel's face as he stared at him. It was so faked that he knew Emmanuel was pretending. Emmanuel's face was filled with such dismay that was closer to fear. Peter now felt a little dizzy from lack of sleep and exhaustion. He felt enraged but for a different reason. He had studied Solomon carefully, and watched his every statement. He had cunningly led him to tell his story. He had felt that Solomon did not wish to live longer on earth by letting his emotions control him. Maybe there was something wrong with him, he reasoned.

"How could you let a woman control your emotional realm like this?" he asked Solomon. He could no longer keep quiet. Emmanuel lowered his face at the question out of shame. It was an unexpected question.

"A woman dedicated to a river goddess? Is that the kind of woman you'll want to spend your whole life with? Remember they say no one can carries fire against his heart without burning his clothes," Peter said.

Solomon's face fell.

"Are you helping me or not?" Solomon asked unabated. Despite his being a choleric, Solomon overlooked and forgave Peter for meddling in his emotions because Peter was going to be very helpful to him.

"Are you helping or not? See, all we need you to do is to help us keep him out of luck, charms, please," Emmanuel pleaded .

By then, all the feelings of fear had passed away from Solomon, and he had told himself that next time he would ask this Peter of a man questions and he wouldn't want to answer him straight, then he would turn his searchlight elsewhere. Of course there should be no repetition of every statement made. He said to himself that what happened had happened. It was his mistake to fall in love with a woman he had known nothing about. Again, he tried to balance his thoughts on not feeling guilty, but he was worried for everything.

Solomon took a look at his wristwatch. The hour was late for him to go to office. If he continued like this, he wouldn't make a good corp member. He became jittery and glared at Peter.

"Listen to me my good friend. What you're about doing has long repercussions I think you've not thought of. One, a medicine man is a spiritual man with principles, " Peter said trying to make Solomon see reason why he should back out from this senseless mission. But, he whom the gods want to kill ,they first make deaf.

The statement sounded a clear warning to Solomon again. It crossed his mind that now was another time for him to drop this idea of marrying this lady and get along with a real life partner. But he spoke no word. Peter assumed his silence to mean that Solomon's mind was made up on saving his girlfriend.

"I must tell you that I'm convinced that you're not ready to leave that girl. So, drop your number with me and I'll give you a call tomorrow's afternoon," Peter said.

"Here is the map of the village in case you would want to go to the village to see things for yourself," Emmanuel said and handed a piece of paper he had collected from Solomon to Peter who took it and left immediately without a word.

"Do you think he will accept the offer?"Emmanuel asked Solomon on their way out.

"He's a very sensitive man. He never considered anything about money. But I think he will," Solomon said . By that time, they had gotten to where their car was parked. They entered the car, Solomon on the engine, and drove into the highway.

FOUR

Very early that morning, Solomon stood by the side of a gutter at the back of his house brushing his teeth. Something he had always done inside, usually in the bathroom. The next thing he saw was Emmanuel with a hand phone waiting consciously for a call they had expected yesterday's afternoon. He had managed to convince Oluchi that after that week, things would cease to be ugly.

A minute past nine o'clock, the phone rang and it was Peter. He told them to turn in immediately. With the address he gave to them, it would take them up to thirty minutes to get to the hotel. And to think that Solomon had not taken his bath.

"I will be fast," he said.

As he came out from the bathroom, Oluchi stood on his way.

"This thing is not the way you see it," she said in tears. But Solomon did not really understand. She wanted to say something, maybe, do something or explain something.

"I said it's going to be all right," Solomon promised. He was not in the mood for love and petting. He believed he had not enough time to fix all he was planning for. He took the corner side and went inside his bedroom. He quickly put on a red T-shirt and a pair of black trousers. He had a quick spray of perfume, took his sunglasses and left. Oluchi followed him with tears running down her face. She assumed that the plan might take another pattern or maybe something was going to go wrong afterwards. She continued following him until he turned and looked at her.

"I will come and pick you for lunch," he said to Oluchi who rather put her arms round his waist and held him tightly with her eyes closed. More tears rushed down. Solomon went closer to the window to check the weather which told him how fast he needed to be.

"In few days to come, we will be forgotten. Yet, both of us will live in a kingdom far away," Oluchi said and bent her head. Yet Solomon would not want to listen. She removed her arms around Solomon to let Solomon go. Her mind went somewhere else. Something was seriously kicking in her mind. Life came to mean nothing to her because everything in it had brought her troubles. It had been useless. "I feel like we're waiting for tomorrow but today has waste away," she cried. Nothing that she had worked for and earned meant a thing to her. Because she knew that she did not belong here-in this kingdom. Though she was not alone in it. But Esther would be waiting for her, and some other people she could willingly bring on board to live in a kingdom very far away with her.

It was said that Oluchi would die but she would not be dead. And all her real mission was to go with souls as many as were willing to follow her. She wasn't regretting, but love was tearing her apart and hindering her mission. She would want as many people as she could get on board and Esther and few others had already gone ahead.

"As long as I live, everything I do will bring joy and happiness to us," said Solomon who was almost at the door on his way out. He didn't even bother to decipher the meaning of Oluchi's words: " *In few days to come, we will be forgotten.*" That was her mission; and not even a powerful deliverance would thwart that mission. The mission must be accomplished. Here was a terrible thing she had felt since in her life. A man had slept with her and warned her never to see her close to his house again. The man had said to her: "Your friends are lesbians and sometimes you behave like one." Then the man mistakenly called her a lesbian and told her that marine spirit was possessing her.

There were powers people should learn how not to play with. Such powers as that of lesbianism, homosexuality, and masturbation. The unpleasant powers of sex were the one consuming every man's soul. The consequences carry unbearable touch that would affect all the episodes of life with time. The next story she heard about the man who called her a lesbian was that he had died in a car accident. Oluchi felt she knew the reason. Esther had died in a car accident and she felt she knew the reason too. Those ones had gone on board. If only we care enough for the living, never will people die. Why Solomon still existed till that moment was because there was true love. Oluchi went over to him again. There was something captivating about her eyes. She slid her arms around his neck. It comforted Solomon just to feel her arms around him .Just for a brief moment, Solomon surrendered to the pressure of her warm body, but then, with a conscious effort, he shoved her away. What she wanted to do to him- it would only take God's intervention to extricate himself from it. She put her head at one side and stared lovely at him.

"I love you my dear Solo. I'm greatly in love with you," she said softly.

Solomon stood, looking at her. He admired her.

"What is keeping you Solomon?" Emmanuel shouted from where he was . Solomon smiled and said; "My love, I will see you when I come to pick you for lunch."

* * *　　* * *

Emmanuel was standing by the car waiting for Solomon when his gaze shifted to an old man who was crossing over to the other side of the road. Immediately, what came to his mind was that any day from that day, they were going to meet an old man, walking with a stick, looking exhausted and physically weak just like the one he just saw.. Fear gripped Emmanuel.

The wall clock on the wall showed ten minutes past eleven o'clock when they entered the building.

"He will be here," Emmanuel said to Solomon who was looking

worried.

In the lounge, they could hear footsteps approaching but they did not turn.

"Good day gentlemen," Peter greeted sitting down on a long vertical chair opposite them.

There was a moment of silence in the room as Peter looked around to see if anybody spotted him coming to the place. When he was sure there was no familiar face around there, he said; "I will do it."

The short statement changed Solomon's countenance. His furrowed brow became relaxed. Emmanuel understood and grinned.

"Time is coming when people will go to bed in peace and wake up in peace," Solomon cheered. He could not hide his joy. He relaxed back on his chair. In his mind, he extended more thanks to God than what was seen in his physical appearance.

Peter looked Solomon straight in the eyes and said to him. "I don't blame you for your shortcomings. I understand your concern. This is what you must know and do. You're fighting a principled man. He's got ways. He neither sleeps at night nor in the day. His charms are always around him. If you want to kidnap this kind of man, you really need some searing exposure of his powers," Peter informed.

Solomon wondered. He could get that one from Oluchi, he felt.

"You can't do this if you don't know how to pray to God, so start learning," Peter advised.

Solomon smiled. "Is that all?"

"If that's how you feel about it, then we can do it," Peter said.

"Thanks man," Emmanuel said with a handshake.

"We have to go," he said.

"Ok," Solomon responded.

When Solomon opened his eyes the next morning, it was already 8 o'clock. He stood up from the bed and stared at the pack of cigarettes and the bottle of whisky on the floor. The thought of the medicine man made him kick his leg on a side stool and a glass cup half- filled with whisky wine landed on the floor. The shattering sound woke Oluchi up and she sprang on her feet. She stared at it for a while half asleep.

"I'll fix it," she said .

"What the hell were you thinking?" She grumbled.

All kinds of thoughts ran through Solomon's mind that he couldn't speak. He wondered if it was because he was going to do something great that day. Oluchi came in with a long scrubbing brush which she used on the floor.

That morning, when Emmanuel finished what he was doing, he went and sat outside because he didn't want to see Oluchi's face. Lately, he had noticed a strange coldness in her behaviour towards him. Peter's last statement, "No one carries fire against his heart without burning his clothes" echoed in his ears. Fighting a principled man was one thing he never thought possible. He was keeping counts of time left for them to go down to Umualamaeze village in search of the former kingmaker; and perhaps, to locate the shrine. When he came inside the house, he looked at Solomon for a short while and said, "It's time."

Time to go, time to do, time to show up. And suddenly, a great fear arose within him again. This time, it was the fear of being apprehended by the police and not for the medicine man.

The two friends hurriedly left home before eleven o'clock to meet the time Peter had given to them. If there were too much troubles in getting the car from Zik"s Avenue where they had picked

Peter to the village, Solomon would be held responsible as he was the one behind the wheel. Peter ordered Solomon to stop for them to change the vehicle's registration plate-number few minutes after they had left Enugu.

When they got to the village, just few kilometers before the shrine, Solomon's phone rang.

"Hello!" He said as he picked the call.

"I am half human, half spirit, a burning flame. Don't say I did not warn you," the caller said and the line went dead.

Solomon began to sweat. His hands were shaking.

"Who's this?" He asked. There was fear in his voice.

Emmanuel sensed that all was not well and became frightened.

"Who was that?" Emmanuel queried looking worried.

Solomon would not want to tell them. He felt he would put their mission in jeopardy and there was nothing to worry about the question Emmanuel had asked. Peter did not say anything. He was looking out through the window. Then suddenly, he ordered in a loud voice; "Stop here."

"Here will be good to hide the car. There is a narrow link somewhere there," he pointed with his finger.

Solomon moved the gear from drive to reverse and then, turned his head backwards, marched down the paddle to steam the engine, and stopped.

"Who called you?" Emmanuel questioned again. Anxiety was written all over him in bold letters.

"Just a friend. The call was just a reminder that I should go and check my name at the National Youth Service Secretariat for skill acquisition registration number," Solomon said to steady his voice and calm Emmanuel down. He tried very hard to cover up his fear even though he was sweating profusely. He was scared that if he tell the truth, his friends spirit would be dampened and that was what he didn't want at that stage when his plan was almost near completion. What they were about to do was his only hope of getting Oluchi out of initiation. Whoever it was that called him on the phone sounded really serious. But what could he do? He had already gotten to the bridge so the best thing he could do was to cross the bridge.

The three men got down from the car and began to walk. Emmanuel ensured that he stayed in the middle. He had never been so afraid in his life. He had the eerie feeling that something awry was going to happen but he kept moving.

"That's em," Peter said as he pointed at a tree. He brought out a small Bible from his pocket, did the sign of the cross with it , and put the Bible back in his pocket.

The place was made of local materials like a local fine-art studio. There were too many inanimate objects around the big tall tree called Bumu Iroko. A red cloth covered the entrance of a small hut which looked like a small dirty cave. Everything in that environment was dull and untidy.

"Do not fear him," Peter warned sternly.

Then turning to Emmanuel, Peter said; "Take."

It was a light stone he had picked from the floor.

"Use it to destroy the altar" he instructed.

"And you," he said pointing at Solomon whose clothes were already soaked with sweat, "you'll help me to carry him."

He managed to break free a little; waiting to see the medicine man on the floor. He looked around to make sure nobody spotted them. The place was so dark that only the person inside could see clearly. Their fear then was how to go in so that the man would not see them first. Emmanuel was assigned the duty of going in first to hit the skull that was hung on the shrine. Peter warned him that he should be very careful because his hand might hang in the air.

While they were still battling with the best way to attack, a man

43

in a red gown came out from the altar and startled them.

"Welcome my children," the man said. He had white designs like local tattoo all over his body. He was not a young man. He was somehow naked without the long garment. He began to sing some songs in his native tongue.

Solomon and Emmanuel were afraid but Peter wasn't. He knew that if they didn't make any move the man would make a move. So he rushed to the old man to hit his head , the old man turned, and Peter landed him a big stone on the head and the man fell on the floor.

"That's that," Emmanuel mumbled and began to hit the shrine with the stone Peter gave him. First of all, he brought down a molded statue in the shrine. Solomon had to do something now. He started destroying the whole place. Maybe Peter had reasons not to bring the car closer but they had got to use some fuel. In a twinkling, the little dear place that looked like a cave became very open and vandalized.

"Give me a helping hand Solomon, will you?" Peter said as he tried lifting up the old man .

Emmanuel quickly ran to the car and picked a gallon filled with fuel while Peter and Solomon carried the old man to their boot.

"Hurry! Hurry!" The two men shouted to Emmanuel because if Emmanuel had failed to handle the altar, they would be in for a big trouble. Peter was worried but would not want to show it. The old man might be dangerous and kill them all. So, he went back to the altar and set it ablaze.

"Go! Go! Go! Let's leave this place!" He shouted in a loud, wheedling voice. They never thought whether the man would be all right there in the boot of the car. They were in a haste to move away from that place. So they entered the car and Solomon drove off hurriedly. No noise was heard until they moved out of the heart of the village.

After about twenty to thirty minutes drive from the village,

Solomon's heart started beating with fright when he remembered that there was a medicine man in his boot. If anybody had spotted them, they would be in trouble. He equally remembered police check-points- and to think that none of them thought about that. Solomon then understood the need for a very quick plan rearrangement. His hands moved round the wheel as he thought of what next to do. He was pretty tensed. He looked at his wristwatch. They still had plenty of time and many miles to cover.

Peter had telephoned and reserved a room at a small hotel that he had once stayed in Zik's Avanue which was on the outskirts of the city. At least, he was certain nobody would spot them there easily. He was really a good programmer. Solomon began to slow down as that was where Peter had arranged to get down. He dared not show himself and he had ironed out every detail for them. Every instruction he programmed was still intact by then. Nothing had changed.

The road was deserted because it was raining. Solomon hated rains but, that day he was happy that it was raining. At least, it would keep the police off the road.

"Get changed!" Peter ordered the two men.

"Did you hurt him badly?" Emmanuel queried as he changed his clothes hurriedly.

There was a small black polythene bag behind the driver's seat. Emmanuel stretched his hand, grabbed it and handed it to Peter.

"That's the money."

"Hurry up, time is running out," Peter advised as he alighted from the car.

As soon as Peter alighted and took to the airport road, Solomon reversed the car and hit the road again. Just then the rain began to pour down heavily. Solomon remembered the old man in the boot of his car again and his heart skipped. He became very nervous.

They arrived the already booked hotel by twelve minutes past seven in the evening. By that time, it had stopped raining but it was still drizzling. Solomon parked his car and the two friends came out . Then, their trouble became how to carry the old man to his room where he would stay for four days without being queried by the hotel attendants. Solomon lost himself in a thought of how best to handle the old man without being noticed. He had the drugs Peter brought for them to give the old man so he won't awake up for three days in his pocket. He looked at Emmanuel to see if he could get any help and was marveled at how the trouble had changed Emmanuel's physical appearance, and how familiar they were becoming with the dirty act of kidnapping. The crinkles at the corners of his eyes and his wrinkled skin emphasized their troubled situation. The two friends could not hide the fact that they were stressed out because it was all over them. But they were still the same Solomon Okafor and Emmanuel Ibe everybody knew and loved once.

"Let's wait till ten at night," Emmanuel suggested.

Solomon nodded, "Good idea!"

They went down the street of Zik's Avenue and entered a small bar. It did not occur to them that somebody could spot them around there. When it finally hit Solomon's mind, he had been spotted by Anthony his former classmate back in school days. He felt very uneasy as he shook hands with Anthony who was in police uniform. Emmanuel lowered his face on the floor and minded his drink. All his doubts about this kidnapping came up in his sub-consciousness again but he waved off the doubts especially now that everything had worked out as planned. The only thing that remained was for Oluchi to go for the deliverance and things would become normal, and Solomon would become a happy man again. Even the medicine man would be taken to church for deliverance and everybody would be happy again.

"I'm on patrol duty tonight. I just came here to buy some things," Anthony said, smiling.

"That's cool, man. I also came here to get some refreshment. You know how it's been, but I think I'll be in my tent. This rain had vowed not to stop," Solomon said as he signaled Emmanuel to get up.

"See you some other time my good friend."

"That's all right," Anthony said. He was not convinced that all was well with Solomon. His instinct told him that something was not just right. That was not the Solomon he used to know. The Solomon Okafor he just met was damned too old; looked too unkept and too dirty for someone serving his fatherland. He looked too frustrated to be the same Solomon Okafor he once knew who always exuded confidence. He wanted to do some catching up, but Solomon was avoiding the idea of chatting under a weather like that. He stroked his beard and watched Solomon and his friend stagger out of the bar with uneasy footsteps. Anthony tried to reason like a cop, pushing aside the fog of friendship and some memories of the past. He assumed an unresolved feeling and a need to be careful. He only came to the bar to buy something. "Well, there is no pot of gold at the end of rainbow," he breathed.

It was remaining forty-eight minutes before the clock strikes ten but Solomon could no longer wait. He needed to get back home and rest. So he went and opened the boot. The old man stared at him with his eyes widely opened. Solomon stared back at him. But the man's sharp eyes were suspicious as Solomon studied the eyes; some was wrong.

"No!" He screamed and quickly flashed the torch. He avoided the man's eyes, and checked his hands which were very cold. It wasn't weather. Something went wrong. He closed the boot and was contemplating what next to do when Emmanuel who was keeping a watch at the gate appeared.

"What is that? I heard your voice. Do you need a hand?" Emmanuel asked.

Solomon wouldn't want to believe what he had just seen.

"Yes," he said. He breathe was heavy and his heart pounded. He opened the boot again and was startled to see that the old man was lying on his back. What is really this? Solomon flashed the torch as he looked at the red gown, the short legs and the small feet was rested against a gallon of engine oil.

"What a mess! What is this?" Emmanuel shouted.

"Get your voice down. What do you think it is?"

"We're stuck with this old man!" Solomon rock bottom in his plans immediately. He began to crack under the strain of the whole thing. it was all over him. The old man seemed a spirit now, fatter and very tense. Emmanuel stood there looking at the dead man. Medicine man is dead?

"What do we do now?" he asked.

Solomon took out his handkerchief and wiped off sweat from his face. He lit a cigarette and inhaled deeply.

"We're leaving this place at once."

"Jesus Christ!" Emmanuel shouted as he was looking at the dead man. He was still astounded.

The street was silent as Solomon began to drive. Across the roadway were lights on the windows of many houses. They drove down to the expressway. Both friends were having an experience, a lecture they never paid for, an idea they never would have bought. In this not-changing particular way, everything kept crawling to them. Part of Solomon was alert while the other part was so disheartened. Emmanuel ran his hands up and down his arms as he tried to quell the fear and panic inside him.

"Violence isn't romantic," he reasoned.

"This is first murder," Solomon felt as he reasoned it, shaking his head ruefully.

"Where are we going?" Emmanuel probed.

"I got plans," Solomon answered. This reply turned up some hope in him. The time was 10:30pm. Outside, it was still raining. He slowed down as he wouldn't want to be spotted for over-speeding. If anything happened and the cops spotted them, they would be in jail.

Solomon hadn't had time to think about Oluchi. He neither told her that he would be coming late that night nor went to work that day. He tapped the steering wheel as he thought of the next thing to do.

There was a signboard with designs of led-lights fifty kilometers away. Solomon drove down the road.

"Is that a fish farm?" He asked looking at the signboard. There was a little sign of excitement on his face.

"I got an idea," he said.

"What's that?" Emmanuel asked.

Solomon slowed down the car, and pulled over.

"I want to dump this corpse in that car," he said to Emmanuel as he pointed at a car parked across the road.

"No, we could be spotted," Emmanuel retorted, "besides, it will give the cops more facts to investigate us and they may close in on us. I suggest we take him back to his village so that his people will not alert the police to look for him."

Solomon nodded in agreement. "That's true. Call Peter now. I think he needs to know of this latest development."

"That's right," Emmanuel concurred, "he really needs to know."

After a minute of delay, Emmanuel was able to get Peter on phone.

"This is Emmanuel," he said, "listen carefully, we could be in trouble. I can tell you that the old man is dead."

"What!" Peter shouted over the phone.

"What are you guys doing about it?" He queried.

"We're trying to put him back on the track where we had picked him from," Emmanuel responded.

"I understand. How is Solomon?" Peter inquired.

"He's behind the wheel."

"There are two things you must know. Don't let anybody spot your car in the village. Then, do not fear anything. Fear could jeopardize your mission. Whatever you do, do it fast; no hesitation."

"Okay, thanks man. We'll keep you posted on our movement."

It was still raining and there was no other car in sight as they drove down the expressway. It was as he was driving down the express that Solomon's plans to kidnap a medicine man blew up to his face. Just at the intersection, he spotted a police man standing by the traffic lights in his long raincoat. The lights flicked to red when he was within forty yards away from them. He could turn back but he wouldn't try it. If he had tried it, they would have been doomed. He eased down on the brake; bringing his car to a smooth stand still, thinking on sort of crime he's about doing as the policeman stared at them. He sat motionless trying to behave as if he didn't exist; aware that the policeman was idly staring at them as if he had known what they were about to do.

Truly, the policeman had nothing else to stare at. It seemed as if they were the only three people left on planet earth. The gray neon lights flashed on and off, entirely for everybody's goodness. The heavy yellow moon floated in a cloudless sky and shone down on them. There was no sign of any other car on the long straight wet road.

Solomon stared at the traffic-red and green light. While the red light was glaring; he stared, willing it could change to green. It seemed symbolic to him. It screamed danger to him, and he gripped the steering wheel so tightly that his fingers ached. It was taking longer to change to green.

The policeman cleaned his face with small face cloth, cleared his throat and spat on the road. The weather was cold. The sound made Emmanuel quickly cast a suspicious eye at him. He was swinging his night-stick aimlessly while staring at them. He was a dark, fat, solidly built handsome man with a round face and pointed nose.

Would the light ever change? Solomon was worried, likewise Emmanuel. He was sweating even though the weather was cold. His eyes shifted back to the glaring red warning sign ahead of them. They were truly dedicated, and no matter what the policeman did, they were already dead.

Then, the traffic lights flicked to green.

Solomon took his foot slowly off the brake and with infinite care, he pressed down the throttle; meaning to smoothly move away, doing nothing to incite the policeman's criticism. The car moved forward to few feet, then there was a sudden cracking sound and the car jerked sharply to a standstill.

Solomon shifted the gear from drive to neutral, and then from neutral to drive again. He pressed down the throttle and the engine roared, but the car didn't move. Solomon sat there with panic crawling over him, he knew that at long last, and after years of good service, the gearbox had finally packed up. Some cog had lost their final teeth, and now they are stuck with a cop not too far away from where they were. It was just about ten feet, and a dead body was inside the trunk of his car. Emmanuel looked and saw something coming to their direction.

"What's that?" He asked. He wanted to open the door, maybe to push the car out of the express way. Solomon couldn't move. He was staring at what was coming closer to them- it was a dog poking its nose on the ground. Dogs are very sensitive. They just sat there watching the dog come closer. Solomon gripped the driving wheel not knowing what else to do.

The green light flicked to red again.

The policeman took off his cap and scratched his shaved head. He should be in the east of his forties. He probably had seen everything- bad, rotten crime. He looked as a man who would rather get you into trouble than out of it; yet, he was coming to their direction. Solomon slid the gear level to reverse, hoping he could move the car from the middle of the road, but the reverse gear did not respond.

"Are you guys planning on sleeping here tonight?" The police man queried as he came to them.

"It looks like we've got a burst gearbox," Solomon said. Emmanuel was silent.

"I see! What are you doing about it?" He asked.

"Is there a garage open anywhere nearby?" Solomon asked.

"I'm asking you what you're doing about it," the policeman shouted. There are little drops of rain on his face.

"Get a tow," Solomon said trying to keep his voice under control. He was thankful that Emmanuel did not say anything. He could put them in a mess. Immediately Emmanuel opened his mouth. "Good afternoon sir," he said. Not knowing why he said it but just to say something. Even though it was late at night, the policeman did not catch the joke of fear he was into.

"Good morning my son. How is the car stressing?" He smiled.

"Now, move the thing off the road or I'll book you for obstruction," he ordered in a very harsh voice.

Solomon got out of the car, followed by Emmanuel and they tried to push it, but it was standing there on a slight gradient and they couldn't move it. They pushed until they were drenched in sweat. The policeman stood watching them.

"You guys need some iron in your bones," he said and slouched.

"Okay, relax! You can consider yourself booked, let's take a look at your driver's license," the policeman said. The effort of trying to move the car had left them breathless. Solomon wanted to do fast to avoid the dog sniffing on them, and he was clever enough to pass him his license along with his identity card.

"What's this?" The policeman asked him.

"I am a corp member. I'm doing my National Youth Service programme," he responded.

"Mr. Solomon Okafor?" He said as he looked at the cards. He pushed his cap to the back of his head.

"Why didn't you tell me so?" He fingered the ID doubtfully, and gave it back to him.

"Well, we serve our country right," he said.

"I love my country," Solomon added.

Meanwhile the dog was still sniffing around their car but the policeman did not even notice that. Deep within Emmanuel's heart, he was saying a serious prayer that the dog should just go. Together they shoved the car of the road. The cop surveyed the sagging boot and there was an expression of disgust on his face.

"Do you guys have something in the boot?" He asked.

"No sir!" Solomon shouted immediately, "it's bad shock-obsever,"

"A burst gear? That's going to take a lot of money to fix."

"I guess so." Solomon replied and wished the man would just let them be.

"What are we going to do? We don't dare leave the car in the garage," Emmanuel said.

"Go get a tow first."

"All right. I will soon be back," Emmanuel said and left.

Twenty minutes had gone since Emmanuel left and Solomon was quite worried. As he sat waiting for Emmanuel, he remembered he hadn't any money on him. He closed his eyes; there was something else he saw. *If you dig a pit, you'll fall in it. Knowing how to charm a snake is of no use if you let the snake bite you first.* A car pulled in front of Solomon and he quickly bent his head. "I am finished," he muttered under his breath. He heard the car door opened but he remained still. He did not stir and the person kicked the side window. "Hey, open the door." He knew that voice so he raised his face; it was Emmanuel's. He never expected him to come with a car instead of a tow. Solomon came down from his car and two of them transferred the corpse into the new car. They used a rope to tie his car to the new car. Thereafter, they drove away.

Apart from the problem of ensuring that they were not spotted at the village, how he would fix his car was on his mind too. He was certain Oluchi would be hurt when she realised that the medicine man had gone. The thought of how he would break the news to her weighed him down. Then Emmanuel stopped abruptly, came down, and went over to Solomon.

"Clean up, we have to leave this car here," he said.

"Why? Is it safer here?" Solomon asked.

"There is a mechanic workshop there," Emmanuel replied.

"That is where we'll fix the car tomorrow."

Solomon was rather silent and looked at the direction of the workshop.

"We will go with only that car. No need towing the car to the village," Emmanuel suggested. They untied the rope, parked the car at a corner where it would not obstruct traffic. Solomon walked back to the car, looking very exhausted and horrible. Emmanuel engaged the gear and drove away. Something made a noise on the car floor but they did not take notice. It was a hand-phone. No word was exchanged between the two friends. The road was dark and unskillfully constructed that Emmanuel had to drive with great care. When they got at the intersection of the road that led to

Umualamaeze village, something flashed Solomon's mind and he alerted Emmanuel who switched off the head lamp to get a proper glimpse of what he had seen. A group of armed men were standing in their direction, perhaps, security men. He parked to his right.

"What do we do now?" Solomon asked in a low tone. He was too weak to talk.

"We dare not leave him here. We need the car to go back. Besides, if we dump him here people will look for answers to, *"why he's here,? who dumped him,? when did the person dumped him.?* The only thing we can do now is to get him back to where we'd kidnapped him," Emmanuel advised.

"Not with those people standing there," Solomon said in fear. Emmanuel's fingers were sweating on the wheel. He tightened it up, removed the car from gear-drive to neutral and pedaled down the brake as he thought of what to do. Suddenly, a wave of boldness and fearlessness came over him. He moved his hand on the gear to put it on drive.

"Are you crazy? What do you think you're doing?" Solomon asked, nervously.

There was flash of torch-light directed on them as they got closer signaling them to slow down.

"Good morning gentlemen!" Emmanuel greeted the security men.

"Are you from this community?" One of them asked the two friends.

"Not at all, actually my mother- in-law fell down from her bed last night, so I want to take her to a hospital. This is my friend, Morris," he said tapping Solomon's shoulder. He was careful enough to put his face down so no one could recognize him.

"Okay, you can go," the man said. Emmanuel nodded, engaged the gear on drive, and zoomed down the village. Solomon watched him thoughtfully.

"You have left me breathless a great many time. What is it with you?" Solomon asked heaving a deep sigh of relief.

If Emmanuel did not act like that, perhaps if the security men had refused them, it wouldn't be a difficult thing for them to dump him at a single corner before the intersection. But the cops could easily spot them. There was another house before the place they were going that had light on its windows. It could be dangerous for them to pass through the same place while going back. But just before the empty shrine which stood alone at the corner of the area; there was a black statue of an old man in a red garment. The shrine was still like that so what could an old man be doing there by this time of the night? The old man looked very much like the one they had in their truck. Emmanuel turned off the headlamp and parked the car in front of the statue which now seemed to be a tree. They shuffled across the shrine. The dust got on their shoes and they took the dust into the car as they dumped the dead body. It was not easy for them as it were when they carried him into the boot. The area was deserted. They could swear nobody saw them. From where Solomon was sitting, he looked through the window of the car and saw that the security men were not really out for those going out from the village as they were for those coming in. So they drove away.

"I hope I shall never forget the goodness of the Lord in preserving us through all the dangers we have been exposed to," Solomon said, shaking his head. Nobody remembered the handset again. It was lost in the car.

FIVE

She lay in an old hard mattress on the floor in her natural dress with her legs curved. Her ribs and collarbone were jutted out. Her black silky matted hair was still new. A masculine hand touched lightly on her shoulder. "Oluchi!" A hard voice called. She opened her eyes and struggled up into a sitting position because if she had jumped up in a rush, she would have made a slip.

"Solomon! Is that you?" She queried.

Solomon sat down with her and ordered for drinks. Without saying a word, Oluchi picked up her clothes and began to wear them for she had been without them. She wanted to have some rest, and she did rested a little. Her suspicions were justified. It was the paradox of their lives that as much as Solomon's opinion kept them together, he would always would to be with Oluchi, and Oluchi wished the same; That they would never become accustomed to being separated. Solomon adjusted and still desperately wanted her with him. Each worried incessantly about the other's health and well-being, at times to the point of making themselves ill. It was fate as good as true love.

"Oluchi, I've got good news for you," Solomon said, "you don't have to leave town again seeking for a prayerful man of God. But, Emmanuel and I made a very big mistake last night."

Now, for some reasons, Solomon was still worried about the slip in their plans. He really had to do something. He got Emmanuel into it. But, let him talk, Emmanuel wouldn't let him. He inclined the ability of a spiritual man physically.

"Pick your things, I want us to meet the man of God at Missionary of God Ministry right away," Solomon said.

"So what mistake did you say you and Emmanuel made?" Oluchi asked and sat down in a chair.

"The medicine man is dead," Solomon answered in a very low

voice. He was apprehensive that Oluchi would harm herself. Oluchi closed her eyes to imagine it. It was difficult for her. The last thing she had ever thought in her life: that the medicine man would die like that.

"How did it happen?" She asked and shifted uneasily in her chair.

Solomon didn't want to tell her everything for he was afraid that she might become hysterical and began to scream. He was about to tell her a few things when Emmanuel entered so he didn't say anything again. Oluchi herself needed not to talk about a lot of things again. The death that claimed Esther and many others had been the worst things that happened in many months ago. Solomon was nearly all handsome in Oluchi's eyes. Everything about him was to her liking. He had been welcomed as a hero, cheered by her, and her alone as she might enjoy it. The thought of the dead medicine man would die off in her mind in time to come.

Solomon was a good man. There were people he thought he must meet, things he thought he must do, and things he thought he must know. There were names he thought he must not forget. Such names like Emmanuel Ibe, Esther Nwokoye, Adanna Ikeanyi, Peter Ukachukwu, and best of all, Oluchi Egwuatu. It was a universal opinion of the two friends; of all remarks, that the friendship between Emmanuel and Peter was in the interest of Solomon and Oluchi, to be happily healed of their problems. But, Solomon would not stop thinking of something in particular which was the tree; Bumu Iroko where the villagers would go to offer their sacrifices. With his naked eyes, he saw when Emmanuel set the tree on fire, and the living tree got burnt. So anybody could imagine how amazed Solomon was to discover some hours later, that the tree did not die. Then, with an old dead man standing beside it - that was truly amazing!

* * **   ****   *****

The congregation were shouting; "The Lord is good!" when they got to the ministry. The last person to enter inside the church was Emmanuel for he was the person that locked the car doors. Twenty minutes later, after much had been said about Jesus and deliverance, a lot of hope welled up within Solomon.

The pastor while preaching the sermon, said; "To tell you the truth, the Bible says in Psalms 119 verse 81;

"I am worn out, Lord, waiting for you to deliver me. I place my trust in your words."

"In verse 87, it says," They have almost succeeded in killing me but I have not neglected your commands. I have confidence in you, Lord." A great cheering and shouting by the congregation followed the Bible verse.

"When do we expect to be delivered?" Mr. Solomon asked a man sitting by his right hand but the man did not say a word. It was then that Solomon took a very close look at the pastor who was dressed in a very rich lace material. The pulpit he was preaching from was made with velvet and gold. The altar piece was very rich: little images and crucifixes were strategically placed in conspicuous places. About six candles wax were lighted . A big portrait picture of Jesus Christ in a frame of marble was at full length upon the cross at the alter, in the agonies, and the blood streaming from his wounds. It was placed above the altar. Solomon stayed through the rather long service yearning for deliverance. After the music and chanting by the congregation, Solomon still waited. The whole experience was nothing to Emmanuel. Nothing in terms of what he had seen. Nothing because he felt it does not make a soul for God. Nothing because he felt it was just a waste of time. The music and praises ended, then it was time for the serious issue that brought Solomon and his friends to the ministry. The pastor after marching around for a while halted.

"We have a visitor," he said all of a sudden and stood still. His two eyes were closed, like he was saying a prayer.

Solomon was shocked as he stared at a strange apparition before him and a displayed bold inscriptions; "I AM A HALF HUMAN, HALF SPIRIT, INVISIBLE ALTAR, AND A BURNING FLAME. DO NOT SAY I DID NOT WARN YOU." Just as it came, the apparition vanished into the thin air with the letters. He wanted to tell Oluchi what he saw but decide against it. Solomon was a mortal man who believed that a man must be his own trumpeter. He must ostentatiously publish to the world his own writings with his name. He must get his picture drawn, his statue made. He must hire all the artists in his turn to set about works to spread his name in order to make the mob stare and gape, and perpetuate his fame. But the mood that poured on Solomon seemed to change during his own fight.

"There is a woman here from marine kingdom, a RIVER GODDESS to be precise," the pastor shouted. He did not delay as he walked towards Emmanuel, Solomon, and Oluchi. Emmanuel adjusted a little. Solomon was sitting between Emmanuel and Oluchi. But in his mind, he was between two opposite spirits, God and river goddess. One may be too serious and not good on some occasions, while the other may be too bad and too rigid on some occasions. One may perhaps overlook an instance or mistake integrity for its opposite but the consequences of these may end one's life.

With the passing feelings, Solomon grew extremely disheartened. His one unfailing source of pleasure, the joy of his heart was Oluchi Egwuatu; whom he told Emmanuel proudly was esteemed by all. She was a prominent figure from Umualamaeze village; the daughter of Chief Christopher Egwuatu, the former kingmaker of their land. Chief Egwuatu was a great man indeed. But that was an ugly situation for him who did not bound in philosophy;

and who could not, and would never trim.

"Stand up," the pastor said to Oluchi whose eyes were already misty.

Solomon followed them to the altar. One thing that kept Solomon going was the spirit of fearlessness which he inherited from his father. He maintained a position of impartiality between the man of God and Oluchi. Things done there could not be understood by everyone. It was not what Solomon or Emmanuel had anticipated. It had a stunning effect to common sense. The pastor called on Solomon.

"Young man, take this fish and cut it open."

Solomon obeyed for he was given a plate and a knife with which to carry out the assignment. After a little prayer with Oluchi, the pastor added; "Take out the gall bladder, heart and liver. Keep them with you. The gall bladder can treat a man whose eyes are covered with a white film."

Solomon stood there wide - eyed at the appalling scene.

"Use the liver and heart to burn in your house to chase away the evil spirit. She has an evil spirit from a river," the pastor informed. Turning to Oluchi, the pastor shouted;

"You demons! Leave and never return!"

The congregation began waving their hands, praising the lord. While some were jumping up ,some were dancing a dance of victory over the activities of the evil one. The pastor's raised his hand to the congregation, "hallelujah!,"

"But, before you consummate your marriage with her, both of you must get to pray to the Lord to be merciful to you and to protect you, Solomon. You had slept with her and you need God's mercies to survive it. Do not be afraid. Oluchi was meant for you from the beginning of creation. You and Oluchi will have many children whom you will love so much. So don't worry! The battle is won and over!" The man of God finally said.

Solomon listened with rapt attention to the man of God. He knew that Oluchi would be delivered but there was another thing that bothered him. That thing was destroying him now. He glanced anxiously at the congregation and then to the pastor. As he walked closer to the pastor, he tried to control the unknown feeling surging strongly inside him.

"What was it that was told?" He asked in the hearing of the pastor , "and please to whom?"

The pastor faced the congregation and said; "Go home, in peace. I bless your nights with colours of rainbows. Peace be unto you Mr. Solomon Okafor. What was told was to her parents-not to you."

Air rasped through Solomon's dry throat. His saliva thickened. He looked once again at the congregation who had began to leave one after the other. "Child's fear," he told himself. Solomon thought he needed to know because the fear of danger gripped him more than he had ever envisaged. The pastor ambled away from Solomon to the altar.

"Go home," he said again to him.

Solomon was no sucker. He was no abuser, and he was sure he was not a prisoner too. He had checked and rechecked. But there was some things he had not thought of. Things like those that come when people begin to feel unsettled. Maybe all that happened was to complete the prophecy. He stood for a little while and turned to face Emmanuel who was there looking at them. Though the pastor said that the prophecy that was made was for Oluchi's parents but something in him told him that whatsoever that was prophesied was all about him. He thought he needed to find answers to this disturbing question. He felt he had the right to know what was prophesied.

SIX

On September 14th, Oluchi was at home faced with lots of rigmarole. The new arrangement was exactly what Oluchi had recommended; and the idea was to leave Solomon feeling more miserable than ever. Solomon had been ill for the first time since he got to know Oluchi. Seven days after the real deliverance, he had suffered a very bad cold. He tried to cure himself in conventional method of walking ten miles a day in the sun. Although he had clearly indicated that his news should be one of those chosen to be untold, neither to his father nor to his people at all. Later that day, having received no further news on Oluchi about demons and evil spirits, Solomon told Oluchi to buy drugs for him. He had fever during the day and sweated at night. A symptom he was sure was of an approaching death.

"I know I will not die," he once told Emmanuel.

Minute by minute, Solomon hurried to where Oluchi was and peered through the curtains. On the floor, he saw a distinct outline of a human foot neither too long nor too small to be Oluchi's. He looked again but he just couldn't understand.

"Oluchi!" He called out a little. His voice trembled with uncertainty. Emmanuel saw what made Solomon trembled and smelled danger. He trembled at the thought of these magic and terrors. Human footprints following an identical path of one another down the stairway. Oluchi had gone to buy drugs so whose footprints were on the floor? Obviously not hers, it was a male foot together with one that could be said to be Oluchi's. "Where has she gone to?" Solomon wondered. On that particularly sweltering Tuesday afternoon, during which Solomon appeared never to have had a better life all his life, he worried that he was dying. He was not sick but he was dying little by little in his physical appearance. It could have been better if Oluchi hadn't told him what was told to her parents about him sleeping with her.

Oluchi's actions towards him told him more than she intended to. They told him that the urge was there. He would suffer the same fate as Chief Egwuatu had suffered for sleeping with a daughter of a river goddess, that curse would cause him his death. Not even deliverance would help. What he did was to exchange his life with hers. Oluchi would still die in time to come. That was the prophecy.

KINGDOM FAR AWAY

The tree was still standing there fourteen days after the shrine was burn and the death of the medicine man. It was still alive. It did not die. A saying in Igboland has it that one could run but could not hide. To Oluchi, what happened to the medicine man was to fulfill all prophecies. It was written before she was born. It was told to her parents. So they knew it. Oluchi knew it. The fact was that Oluchi was projected. She was never born. Twelve days back, something had happened at the shrine that crystallized the fact. Some policemen went to there to investigate the death of the medicine man, Richard. On getting there, they saw him stood beside the same tree.

"That's him," said one of the police officer holding a paper in his right hand. Out of fear, they retraced their footsteps back to where they left their Toyota 4x4 truck. They did not imagine it could be a nightmare because a sudden sound was made at its appearance. The sound was light, yet too serious to be made by something intended godly. They retreated because they all admitted the guilt for trespassing. Nobody prays to die in the line of duty. Supposing they forgot what they saw and went back to understood it well. After all, a dead dog do not bite. So they regrouped and went back. What would they have to present to the office if they hadn't gone back? Nobody would believe them if they told the story of what they saw. They walked through the narrow shortcut in a small forest that linked to the shrine, struggling against the odour and against the spirit to run back. They were on full alert on any likely eventuality. They would like to see the walls of thorns. And they would also like to get to the root of another mystery which was unraveling what other mission the dead man had again on this planet earth. They need not be reminded that the mystery would be hard to solve. Few minutes before they stepped into the shrine again, great fear enveloped all of them. Perhaps, in no distant time, it seemed that everything was going to be made clear at last. Strange sounds were heard but they did not run because they could not. Was it because of long narrow thorny path? Not at all. It was as a result of fear. They had imagined the thorns would disappear at the cause of the noise. They paused there for seconds. Or was it a miracle that they were still alive? One of them made a noise with his foot marching on the ground as he stepped forward before them all.

"Ancestors of our land, we greet you," he said with little fear in his voice. "We are here to investigate the death of our father, Richard."

There was no response. Then He led the way and others followed. God's blessings were never the same thing. What he did was what his father told him. To appreciate the power of everything around him. Perhaps, it was the power of appreciation that kept everything motionless. They thought they heard some noise and wondered where the noise came from. They continued moving round the tree to figure out something, but recalled that some people had been there before them to carry out the corpse. The business became a more interesting one. It would now be a one-on-one questioning. If any offered an answer, they would take.

* * * * * * *

Solomon felt better after taking the drugs. They were on long hot hiking from the top of the first dune. They rested at the top of the dune for some moments before they continued with their journey. As they walked, their feet stuck fast in the thick mud so they were forced to lean forward as they walked. It was a difficult traverse to the lake. But Solomon and Oluchi had no complaints. It was a quiet place with only the wind and the swish movement of the dune grass bringing sounds to their ears.

After a long walk side by side, Oluchi sat on the floor. Solomon took her hand and kissed it. Her breath caught another quiet little sigh as she let him take her over. As she sailed over her smooth, gentle waves of pleasure; under his hands, she was like an egg, willing to lay herself open for whatever he could give or take. The beach became very cold so she arched him once again wrapping herself around him that they sat, locked together. This was time to dismiss. Such time had come when all that one thought would affect only one's emotions. They stood up one after the other to go home. If Solomon had not stood to go home, Oluchi would have dragged him up. As they went, Solomon would from time to time reach out and stroked her hair tenderly. And each time, feelings of love filled his soul. The caressing was so soft to her skin that at the moment took a dreamy hue that made it easy to be tender. He yearned to cherish her at home, and he wondered if anyone ever had. Instead of seeing her as competent, clever, practical, and smart; he had wondered if anyone had ever shown her how precious she was. He whispered sweet nothings to her as he eased her over to the other side so he could open the door.

They entered the room and headed to their bed. As soon as their bodies touched the mattress, his hands began working all over her. Considering her as delicate and fragile, he handled her tenderly like diamonds. He was really cherishing her. Her breath became heavier. There was a long, lush kiss that sent warm thrills through their veins and sent them pulsating with an overwhelming excitement. Oluchi aligned herself as they united in a just cause. Mouth met mouth urgently, breathing quickened as the air went misty. Need welled up inside her, throbbed like a wound, and spread like fever. That thing continued racing inside her. She murmured his name over and over again. She pushed him back, as she straddled him and cupped his hands to meet her body all over. She guided him inside her and captured him in all that velvet heat. He could feel the counter of her heart, the shivers along her skin, and the taunt brace of it as she set to ride him. Then she lean forward, her hair hanging down to cover both her face and his. She anchored her hands on his shoulders, dug her fingers in and murmured: "Why me?" Her hips charged like lightning, shooting sparks of shock through his blood. The pleasure stormed through him now, whipped by her energy. She threw her head back, crying out, "Come… come… this is sweater than wine." Then, her honourable body wetted and she screamed out, "Oh, I love you!" She opened her eyes to and met his. Thin warm sweat dribbled down. Solomon had been condemned. She squeezed his nipples with her two hands and Solomon opened his mouth.

"This is me," she continued.

SEVEN

It seemed like years ago when she came into the world. Solomon's life had just been redeemed. The prophecy had come with harder days. What Solomon did was to promise to be responsible for a stranger's debts. He acted as surety for a stranger and now his life was on line for the payment of the debt. He knew things had not been straight and he was nervous. As he entered his house, he heard an eerie noise and he became scared. The silence that followed immediately got him even more scared. The long narrow stairwell that led to the sitting room was splashed with water and that made the passage not to look like the silver colander it used to look like. Solomon made use of the doormat to wipe the wet shoe. He expected the shuffling noise to tell Oluchi that he's home. To this end, he had expected that Oluchi would come out to welcome him. Then, rather, he believed that she was asleep; or better, that she was away from home.

"What about that sound?" He wondered.

The silence suddenly became very oppressive. Its weight laid upon him like a dense mass. Solomon still did not quite realize what was happening to him, but the heavy dense mass that weighed him upon his heart was more persuasive than any argument. Oluchi was not at home, yet the door was left open. Maybe she didn't go far. With a stealthy movement, he stepped into the house . But this is my house, he reasoned, as he tried to drive away the fear in his heart. He opened the first door, yet there was nobody. He could swear that the eerie sound he heard earlier came from his house or was he hallucinating, he wondered. But, there was something that made him believed that whoever was in the house hadn't gone far. He took a close look at the door, it was not tampered with, the house was not burgled. His suitcase was so important to him that he had not dropped it even though it was heavy so he headed straight to his bedroom. Few steps to his bedroom, the thought of whether he had been visited by the men of the underworld crossed his mind again. But he opened the bedroom door and quickly switched on the electric light bulb. It was only when he saw Oluchi lying in the bed, still in her blue flowered gown that he heaved a deep sigh of relief.

"Oluchi, how could you sleep with the entrance-door opened? You should have at least closed the door before sleeping," he said, smiling. He kept his suitcase on top of the wardrobe, went over to where Oluchi lay.

"Hey! Wake up! I'm home," Solomon said as he undid his buttons. Solomon was surprised that Oluchi was still sleeping not minding all the noise he was making so he bent to kiss her, then he saw something- Oluchi's two eyes were widely opened!

NO ONE CAN FIX THE BOUNDARIES OF THE EARTH

Solomon's life had just begun. He took two slow steps forward and peered at her. The colour of her skin had changed. It was darker. It showed very clear on her face. Greatly frightened, he stepped hurriedly back. He stood there for several minutes. He was sure he was dreaming. Yes, it was all a dream! Was he? So, it was real! It was death! He wondered as he tried to accept the fact that Oluchi had just passed away. He sauntered into the sitting room to look for Oluchi's phone. Sweat had formed on his brow and his hands too. He was fidgeting. He was both dazed and scared. What really happened? What could have happened to her? Oluchi was hale and hearty when he left that afternoon. She neither complained that she was sick nor did she look sick. He had just been gone for two hours, forty-five minutes! Did somebody kill her? He wondered. Then a sudden horrible thought dropped into his mind that made his heartbeats sound like a collision of two metals.

"What would I tell the police if they come here? I'm sure they would pin the murder on me. Everybody knows Nigerian police don't look for answers; they always have answers. They don't investigate; they look for stories. They don't look for suspects; the witnesses are already suspects. But, what did death see in my friends? Why has death decided to pitch his tent near my dwelling place? Doesn't death have any where else to go than to attach himself to myself?" Solomon lamented bitterly.

At that moment, it dawned on him that Oluchi was not meant for him. The most disturbing thing was Oluchi's people. How would he trace them?

"What do I do with this?" Solomon asked himself. Hot tears continued streaming down his face, they were hot, he could feel it.

A knock on the main door alarmed him and made him remembered the phone in his hand so he dialled Emmanuel's number, placed the phone on his ear and moved to answer the door. With the phone still placed at his right ear, he pleaded, "Just come now. I need an assistant. There are decisions to make and I need a seconder. If you come and I've gone, just come straight to Leeds hospital." Solomon opened the door. Standing on the door was Adanna. He was surprised to see her.

"Please, come in; there is real trouble here."

What do I do? My car is still with the mechanic. And I need a car to take her to the hospital for confirmation," Solomon cried.

"To the hospital? Who are you taking to the hospital? Is Oluchi all right?" Adanna asked

"I can't say. Come and see," Solomon said and led Adanna to the bedroom.

"Oh my God! What happened to her?" Adanna shouted and threw herself on the ground.

"Oh my God! This is not true! I can't believe it!"She kept wailing. Solomon felt really bad. He went to Adanna.

"Stop crying, things will be all right. I know there are better days ahead," he consoled her with unsteady voice. On hearing those words, Adanna wiped her tears. With her two misty eyes fixed on him, she asked; "What really happened to her?" "How did this happen? "When did this happen?"

That was when it dawned on Solomon that he was yet to grasp the reality of what had happened. With just one unsteady blow, the person he loved passed away; yet he couldn't cry. He knew something was definitely wrong with him.

"But, I spoke with her in the morning. I was with her in the morning. Now ,she's gone," Solomon said in a low voice and began to arrange the room. He used a bedsheet to cover the corpse. Adanna stood wondering why Solomon was acting strange. How could he be busy with arranging things in the room when he had just lost the most treasured person in his life? So, she said in a voice laden with anger; " I need an explanation. What happened to her?

Solomon did not sobber. He did not shed tears. He talked very well. Oluchi had told him two days ago to be an example. She had spoke to him saying, *"I am proud to have known you. You are the best thing that has ever happened to me. I wish I could stay but that was what they said to me. They said I would never be delivered. My mother told me so. She said I have supernatural power; and many spirits are following me. The day after the deliverance something happened that bothered just me and me alone because I entered a ministry and called the name JESUS. I was alone at home when you left with Emmanuel. They came to me and told me that the appointed time for me to join them has come. I've been alone in the world, but I was made to understand that I've not been alone. About five minutes after you left, the door opened and somebody came in. He was my husband. He was in faded white garment. He was trying to show me something but I could not understand. He was totally different from other people; and different from the way I had known him. He deposited in me the spirit of a different mind. I never wondered why all these things were happening because I knew it would all happen. It was told from the day I was born that I would die and return like a ghost. My love, never cover your face or eat the food that mourners eat. Do not cry your heart out because of my imminent demise. My mission on earth is fulfilled. I will soon depart from this earth; yet you will hear from me on seventh day after my departure."*

"Oluchi was the only woman I loved," Solomon said to Adanna as he bent down and carried Oluchi's dead body with his two hands. "God forgive me for I have known nothing I have done." He carried his deceased girlfriend through the narrow passage with light-green ceramic tiles. Then he moved into the sitting -room and laid the corpse on one of the couches as he waited for Emmanuel who was to come with a car to take her to the hospital, or perhaps, to the mortuary. More responsibilities await Solomon. His happiness was that he needed an end to all these things; and Oluchi had told him what to do when it all started happening. When Emmanuel finally came, he parked his car closer enough and went upstairs.

EIGHT

Life was not too short. Solomon felt it was not a rehearsal. But, there were few things that were very difficult to understand. An eagle could fly in the sky, a ship could find its way on the sea, a snake could move on the rock, but the most wondrous thing was how a man and a woman fall in love. When a man fell in love or a woman fell in love, they would confess, "I love you" not wondering if they were under a curse. Solomon felt he was under a curse. He had first thought of it, but what he chose to call love blinded him from reasoning very well. It was said that a man must have a guiding God. He must have a wife. He must make, and have children; and he must die in time to come.

"Useless," Solomon said to himself. "Life is useless. we spent nine months in our mother's womb. we haven't spend enough on earth; yet, we spend the rest of eternity in a coffin."

As Adanna listened carefully, she felt it was time to free herself from emotional stresses. She was hurt by her past life; living with the memories of Esther Nwokoye. And now, to join Oluchi's memories to her emotional troubles was frightening to her. Emmanuel's right hand which was placed on her right shoulder gave her soothing feeling. She gladly welcomed the effect the touch gave. The feeling was heightened when Emmanuel asked her in a very calm voice, "How are you doing dear?" She took her eyes away from him as he glanced back at her for she couldn't bear it. She just gave him a tender affectionate smile pretending she was normal. She felt secured anyways. But, for how long and how real? There was a picture of Oluchi on the wall. Solomon had purposely left it there to keep memories. Another one laid horizontally to the TV stand. Adanna sat on the long vertical seat and wished Solomon could remove the pictures from the sitting room and place them in his bedroom.

A knock on the door got Emmanuel wondering who the caller might be as they were not expecting any visitor. But Solomon came out to get the door. Then he stopped. He needed to hear the knock again. Adanna and Emmanuels' eyes were on the entrance too. When the knock came again, Solomon cautiously opened the door.

Two men stood opposite Solomon whose hands on the door were shaking due to only one thing. Another man on uniform stood behind them too, making the visitors three. Solomon made way and the three men stepped into the house, the six eyes darting around the house, looking for what they could tell.

"My name is Robert Jerry. I'm a police officer," one of three men who was in black suit said. When they heard that, Emmanuel adjusted himself while Adanna turned her face away. Fear engulfed Solomon and he felt like making a dart for the door.

"Here with me are my men. We are here on official duty," the man said again. Solomon nodded. "We are looking for one Miss Oluchi Egwuatu. Do you know her?" The policeman asked.

"Yes, I know her," Solomon replied. His voice was unsteady. He released his hands off the door handle and put his door keys into his pocket. He went into the sitting room with the three men. He seemed a bit at ease. Adanna and Emmanuel cast a known look at themselves. The policeman brought out his hands, which all the while had been in his trousers pocket.

"She's needed at the police station for questioning in connection with a stolen car on the 13th of this month. So, may we meet her?" the police man said.

"How do you mean she was connected with a stolen car?" Solomon asked in a loud voice.

"Sir, you have the right to remain silent and provide her; otherwise, we'll charge you for obstruction of official duties and destruction of evidence," the second police officer said.

"Who are you to come to my house to tell me what to do and shout at me?" Solomon barked at the policeman, "this is not Oluchi Egwuatu's house. You know where to find her. This is my house!"

"Solo!" Adanna called.

"No, Adanna. Don't Solo me. This men want to arrest Oluchi," he shouted visibly angry.

"Calm down Solomon, calm down," Emmanuel cautioned. Go and sit down, I will take it from here," he said to Solomon.

"Officers, I sincerely apologize on his behalf. The person you're looking for is dead. The funeral service is around the corner. That man there," he said as he pointed at Solomon, "was his fiancé."

"Fair enough," the senior police officer said and put back his hands into his pocket again.

"This phone was recovered from the stolen car. It recorded that the phone was used to call Oluchi during the day before the night the car was stolen. The sim card of the phone is coded, but we rounded another suspect who told us that the caller told him that his madam wanted him for a job. That madam's name was Oluchi Egwuatu. The name of this suspect is Peter Ukachukwu," the police officer painstakingly explained. "Do you know him?" He asked.

Solomon's countenance changed. He slowly lowered his face. Adanna was confused. She couldn't grasp the drama unfolding before her very eyes. Emmanuel stood tongue-tied and wide-eyed with shock. His face suddenly looked like that of an old hawk. After the debriefing, the police officers left the house. Adanna felt sweat on her feet so she removed her foot wears. She placed her two hands across her chest, nodding her head in anger.

"Can somebody explain to me what those police officers came here to do? What were they saying about Oluchi, phone, stolen car?" She asked, though to no one in particular.

Emmanuel moved closer to Solomon. "Hey man, you never said

anything about the missing phone?" He asked angrily.

Solomon kept quiet. The only thing that was troubling him about the whole thing was that Peter was in police custody. He needed to know what Peter had told the police. If he went to the police station to see Peter, perhaps, the policemen noticed him, he would be in a lifetime trouble. But, if he waited for his freedom, perhaps, for them to free him, Peter might gain grievances over that and expose them.

"What do I do now?" He thought aloud.

Nigerian government had a tough law against car thieves. Not only that, it could lead to the death of the medicine man. Nobody who was accused of car theft and murder escaped a hangman's noose.

"Long time ago, Peter had tried to explain to me why I should not bother my life with this curse of Oluchi but I was adamant. See where it has landed me - a murder suspect! And not just that, being associated with a man who had such a criminal history like Peter is bad enough. I can never exonerate myself from this case," he lamented.

"Nobody blew it! The medicine man could be at work," he mumbled as he turned to Adanna, " I am so sorry for bringing you into this. The truth is that an old man died in our hands while we were trying to kidnap him."

"We? Kidnap?"Adanna asked and looked at the two men in confusion. Emmanuel saw her state and said; "It was not really a kidnap. See, Adanna, you're the strongest woman I have ever seen. But, I can bet you don't have all the strength needed to take in the full story. I don't want the police to mention your name for any reason whatsoever. Solomon and I made a very bad move that landed us in this bad shape," Emmanuel tried to explain. But tears wouldn't let Adanna say a word. She kept sobbing.

"Please take me home," she said quietly when she found her

voice.

* * * *　　* *　　* * * *

The time was 11.53pm, bed time. Solomon lay in the unmade bed like stick of matches in a match-box. *No one lights a lamp and hides under the table instead, he will place it on the lamp-stand so that people coming in may use it to see. Your eyes are like a lamp for the body. When your eyes are sound, your whole body is full of light; but, when your eyes are not good, your whole body will be in darkness. Make certain, then, that the light in you is not darkness. If your whole body is full of light, with no part of it in darkness, it will be bright all over, as when a lamp shines on you with its brightness; you're the light of the world.* Solomon tossed and turned in bed as he tried to sleep. Part of those words sounded again in his hearing, *"You're the light of the world!* He rolled to the other side of the bed. The time was 12:43am. Everywhere was dark. Perhaps, because no electric light bulb was on. Solomon's favourite sleeping position was sleeping by his side and clutching his pillow. Five minutes later, the strong arms of sleep overpowered him and dragged him to the dream land.

Thousands of people crowded on a particular road. That was very unusual. At the small dirty house, at the end of that road, stood a flirtatious young lady. She was staring at Solomon and he was walking quickly towards her. The area was a mixture population of Nigerians and Ghanaians. The young woman stood at the entrance of a particular building. Solomon was awe-strucken as he admired the place. The next moment, Solomon saw himself with the flirtatious young woman again. It was then he clearly saw the woman's flirting eyes. He entered the small dirty house with her and saw himself in a neat room with the woman. Few minutes after the door was closed, the woman began to dance. Drum-beat as she danced like that of the cultural days in African communities. The beating and dancing continued. Nobody was seen beating the drums but the sound of the drums was heard and the woman danced. Solomon stood there. Something that was not familiar with him, yet he became familiar with it. The bedroom grew cold with time, and he began to enjoy her moves. Perhaps, he had fallen for her tricks. He sat down at the edge of a well made bed in the room. The excitement he was getting from watching the dancer overwhelmed him that after a time, he began to nod to the rhythm of the drum beat. The beauty of the dancer's face, the flirtatious smiles, the eyes, the moving hips- he really got lost watching all. The woman made him lay against his back in the bed. She was dressed in overflowing flowery red gown. Soon, she removed her body, uncovering her nakedness. Solomon was still lying in the bed when she went over on him, unzipped his trousers, unbuttoned his shirt and began to caress him with her two soft hands. Then, the woman began to speak slowly;

"We are going to our final resting place! There will be mourning in the streets. The silver chain will snap, and the golden lamp will fall and shatter. The rope at the well will break and the water jar will break. Our bodies will return to the dust of the earth. The breath of life will go back to the Creator who gave it to us. Then, we'll live our lives in a kingdom far away." Then she stopped, giggled and spoke in a voice too husky to be a woman's.

"Remember, SEVEN DAYS!"

An unappealing silence followed.

After few minutes of silence, that soft voice came again.

"This is where the light of the moon, the sun and the stars will grow dim for you, and the rain clouds will never pass away, you're the light of the world!"

Solomon sat up from the bed with a jump. It was all a nightmare. He recognized the city in the dream. It was Umualamaeze village.

He became petrified with fear. He remembered the day Oluchi died and since then, he had been a traitor to himself more than he had ever imagined. He became afraid of everything. He left his room and moved to his sitting room. He looked at the things he had taken enough time to arrange, his eyes rested on the wall as he continued to make meaning out of his dream. They made him a king of a city and he slept with the queen of the city which was Oluchi. Just then, his eyes rested on the framed picture of Oluchi and himself which was hung on the wall of the sitting room. The picture had broken! His eyes widened in fear. Many things really needed explanation. Gradually, the awful truth dawned on him that something visited him last night. His phone began to ring and he picked the call.

"Hello!" He answered weakly.

"Let me guess, you're not in a good mood. How was your night?" The caller asked.

"Fine! Who's this?"

"Chris, from Texas Automobile Management and Process, TAMP," the caller answered.

"Ok. Is the car ready?" Solomon asked.

"Yes sir. I have just finished your work," he replied.

"Ok, I will come along then." Solomon ended the call and dropped the hand phone, but his eyes were still fixed at the picture frame which had been on the wall throughout last night only to be on the floor that morning. He glanced around the room and saw that the next picture after his personal one which was Oluchi's was missing. The picture which he placed on top of the television was no longer there. It gave him an inkling that something was really wrong.

Solomon was worried. His fear heightened. "Who rearranged these pictures? Who took away Oluchi's pictures?" He asked, rhetorically.

When Solomon got to the mechanic workshop, on one particular move he while bringing out his car from the mechanic workshop attracted the attention of passers-by. That move was a display of recklessness and gear selection abuse. Really, it was not a cool move except for those that prefer James Bond driving style. What heightened the drama was that after that action, a man came closer to his car and stood by the left hand door.

"My name is Pastor Williams. I am a man of God," the man said as he offered his hand for a handshake.

Solomon waited to hear him through. He recognized him. He could attest that he had met him somewhere.

"On the eighteenth day from today, you will be no more. You need a serious deliverance," the man said.

Solomon looked at the man very intently. He was convinced the man was certain of what he had said. But he had to be sure he hadn't fallen into the wrong hands.

"This parable you said now, how did it concern me?" Solomon asked the man.

"When you see the cloud coming up in the West, at once you say that it is going to rain and it does, and when you feel the South wind is blowing, you say that it is going to get hot and it does. Hypocrites! You can look at the earth and the sky and predict the weather. Why then, don't you know the present time? Can't you remember your past? With it, you can predict your future." The man tried to explain.

"What!" Solomon shouted. He was confused.

"Trouble! Why do you not judge yourself by your actions? You're in a trouble of a lifetime," the man replied.

The man's words drew Solomon's attention to the fact that there might be a direct correlation between pastors and philosophers in a lesser volume. In fact, it had occurred to him that if he did not learn from this man he might not see him again. He felt cold blood flew through his vein. His heartbeat was pounding. He began to wonder if all that was a religious scam. But he was sure something visited his house last night. Oluchi's picture was missing too. As Solomon took some consolation from his believe that at the end of everything with this man, he would be talking about living a worthful life. Last night was another time he felt so close to death. He was glad that the man of God had already given him an appointment to visit his church for prayers. Solomon recalled that it was only once he stayed out at night; and that was the night of the day his ex-girlfriend slept with his friend. Since they became separated, his life had changed. Cars were coming closer and Solomon needed to get his car out of the way so he wouldn't obstruct traffic. When they had finished their discussion, Solomon engaged his gear to drive, and then, to reverse. All he listened to in his car music player was a song in a music album titled, "Life After Death: if I should die before I wake," by Biggie Smalls (Notorious B I G), released on 25th March 1997, after the death of Tupac Shakur in 1996.

Over the next half an hour, Solomon was driving. The traffic was free. The man's words didn't leave his mind. There was something easy about his happy mood that afternoon. It wasn't forced. It was just flowing naturally. But Solomon couldn't escape the feelings that it was simply a means to an end. All he felt he needed to do was just to make a choice. He entered a building off the road. He had been to that building before, he recalled. This was the same ministry he had been with Oluchi and Emmanuel. He lost confidence immediately but he couldn't go back. He decided to try again so he walked to an entrance, and then waited by the door side to check if he could spot the man of God. There were approaching footsteps which drew nearer and clearer, but Solomon did not stir until a hand rested on his shoulder.

"Mr. Solomon Okafor, this way please," a man said to him.

He followed the man to where the man of God was counseling people. It was now closer to mid-day. Solomon sat on a bench with his head bent. He was in deep thought. There was this deep-seated fear that if he left without seeing the man of God he might not see daybreak. Solomon had been opened to temptation long enough that he knew that if Oluchi was to be alive, he was not sure he would let her go. At a time in his life, he considered it a good idea to see a man of God. That was then when Oluchi was still alive. But, should things go bad enough, it would only end in disaster. He remembered Oluchi's words. *Any woman would see reasons to be thankful for being in your life.*

"Oluchi has gone-dead. She would never come back again," Solomon said to himself, " yet, I'm not even sure that redemption is the next thing. All that matters to me now is this trouble of a life time I'm in. I thought I was having a nice time with Oluchi. I didn't know I was digging my own grave. Now the repercussion of my actions is here with me. The implication of my action is more dangerous than fifty gun shots. It kills slowly. Whosoever slept with a woman dedicated to a river goddess would only be saved by God Himself. People should learn to desist from sex now more than ever" he regretted.

"Mr. Solomon, the Pastor wants to see you," the man said interrupting his train of thought. Solomon thanked him and he left through another door.

On getting to the pastor's office, Solomon knocked, opened the door and went in. He closed the door after him.

"Good day man of God," he greeted and sat down on one of the chairs in the office.

After meditating for a few minutes with his holy book spread in front of him, he looked up.

"Who are you?" The man of God asked Solomon. Solomon wasn't surprise. He was ready to introduce himself but he wasn't really sure of what the man meant by the question. He was still battling within himself on the proper way to answer the question when the man of God threw another bombshell at him;

"Solomon is not your name. Am I right?" he asked.

Solomon could swear he was either not at the place or he was not talking to the right person. How could the man say that Solomon wasn't his name? A name he had bore all these years.

"I'm 27 years old, and all my life I have been going with the name Solomon. So, I'm really surprised at this question," he answered, trying to control his nerves.

"You have no name," the man said and looked away.

"My name is Solomon Okafor; so say my parents!" Solomon protested.

"No, you have no name. What I saw and heard in the vision filled me with pains and terrors. A great deal of pain like that of a woman in labour."

"How do you mean?" Solomon asked.

"What did you do?" He asked.

Solomon kept quiet.

"I see darkness," the man of God continued, "dark secrets, wrapped in mystery, shrouded in illusion. You are not what you seem. You are running away from something. Your are running from your past. But, I must tell you that no matter where you run to or how far you run, you are already in danger. There is a cloud of darkness hanging above you. And it won't be too long before the cloud covers your whole being. I see danger." The man of God paused for some minutes and continued; "I see ... I see nothing. ... You ... You exchanged your life! You exchanged your fate, your great destiny, your shining star, except your face. But I see another face. Yes, I see a face."

"Whose face?" Solomon interrupted anxiously, "is it that of a male, or of a female?"

"No! It's neither that of a man nor that of a woman."

Solomon started trembling in fear. His head began to spin. He had been longing to see this man of God but now the revelations from him brought him nothing but terror.

"Whose face do you see then?" Solomon asked quietly.

"The face of death!" The man of God replied immediately.

"I s-e-e ... death!" the man of God groaned shaking his head in despair.

Solomon's car key, hand-phone, and a pen fell off his hands. He was trembling with fear.

WHEN AN ENEMY PUTS HIS HANDS AROUND YOUR SHOULDER, WATCH OUT!

Solomon's life had become a bold and delicate projection of the eternal into the temporal. He was sure it has ended. There were few things that could never be satisfied. It was the biggest fight Solomon ever had. It was a fate as good as trying to satisfy a woman without a husband or fire burning out of control. He felt he was seriously close enough to the world of the dead. It was just like a kingdom very far away; or rather, he felt he was a living dead and should return to their kingdom. What remained now was half of an extra-time.

"What should I do?" Solomon asked the man of God.

"I see. Who paid your debts?"

"I had no debts," Solomon answered.

"Who did you pay her debts?" The pastor asked.

Solomon hesitated. The truth was that, over the last few days, he had lost a greater sense of reasoning. All he could say was that, "there is fire on the mountain." Now, over the last few minutes they had talked, the faces of each other they had watched, it was just now as the pastor stood to his feet that the real question came out. Solomon turned away his face so that the man of God would not see his tears. More so, he did not want to let out the secret part of his whole fate. This fate was a visitation.

"Her name was Oluchi Egwuatu," he responded, "I don't know a thing. All I know was that people were talking about us. They said things in parables which I didn't understand."

"What is wrong with the world we're living in?" The pastor said and turned his face away for he himself was in tears too and he wouldn't want Solomon to see that.

"When will all this get undone?" Solomon wept.

"A chance has been uploaded for you. There is only one person who will save you from all this."

"You have to bring her mother here," the pastor said.

"Whose mother?"Solomon asked.

"Oluchi's mother." The pastor replied.

"I don't know if I can ever find her."

"You must find her. She has something to tell you."

Solomon's face fell. He knew that even if he was able to locate Oluchi's mother, it would be difficult to convince her to follow him to see the man of God with the fact that he and Oluchi's mother had never been best of friend.

"The connection between madness and evil spirits was experienced by Mrs. Barbra Egwuatu alone. So, she alone could tell the story," the man of God informed Solomon. There was silence in the counseling room. The time had come when things would be given serious attention. But everything still seemed hopeless for Solomon.

"Many are deceived by prophets who promised peace to those who pay them and trouble those who don't. Now, yours has just been redeemed," the man of God said. His words brought a ray of hope to Solomon. Even though time was no longer on his side, he had to set out immediately to go and look for Oluchi's mother.

As Solomon left the ministry and headed to the park, he knew he needed somebody to accompany him to Enugu but he couldn't possibly get any kind of person involved. He had to be discreet on the issue. He equally needed some privacy with Oluchi's mother. Emmanuel was the only person he trusted but he knew it would be difficult to convince Emmanuel to accompany him to go and search for Oluchi's mother. He was sure Emmanuel would no longer want to be involved in anything that had to do with Oluchi considering his behaviour lately. But that was not his trouble. On his way, the thought of not telling Emmanuel kept hitting his conscience for he knew Emmanuel was the only one he could rely on, should any trouble spot along the line. He recalled what happened when he didn't tell Emmanuel about the missing phone and when he didn't tell Oluchi about his plan to kidnap the medicine man. The fear that since he started this journey, none of his plans had ever worked as planned, hunted him. He sighed and resolved to let Emmanuel know his whereabouts as soon as he got back to Enugu.

He got at the bus stop later in the day and as he waited to board another bus that would take him to Area 23, he became worried about how he would convince the woman to follow him to see the man of God. He wished sincerely that he had called Emmanuel. Right from the beginning, there had never been a time she approved his relationship with her daughter. Mrs. Barbra had always loved her daughter. When Oluchi died, she pleaded her to come back because there was no other person to take her position, and play her part in her life.

When he got to Area 23, Solomon took the second walkway into the compound and walked straight to the third flat. He stood before the door and took a deep breath as it dawned on him that he was standing in front of Mrs. Barbra's door. He took another deep breath and knocked on the door. His eyes were on the door when the door slowly opened and a short plump dark woman came out.

"Who are you looking for?" The woman asked in a very harsh tone.

Solomon hesitated. "This is not Mrs. Barbra." He looked stunned, but he soon regained his composure.

"I'm here to see Mrs. Stephanie Barbra Egwuatu."

The woman stood there, looking at him as if she did not understand what he said. Solomon was looking frustrated and helpless.

"Sorry, I can't help you," she said and was about to close the door
.

"Please wait, it's urgent. I really need to see her now; help me please," Solomon pleaded and knelt down. Just then a man in clean white singlet came to the door. When he saw the man, Solomon stood up. He felt relieved when the man offered his hand for a handshake.

"How may we help you, young man? the man asked him.

"My name is Solomon Okafor. I'm here to see my mother- in-law, Mrs. Stephanie Barbra Egwuatu. Please how do I reach her?"

At that moment, a phone rang inside the bedroom. The woman went to answer the phone and left the two men at the door.

"Yes, madam," the woman said immediately she picked up the phone call. After discussing with the caller , she went back to the two men and said to Solomon;

"Find your way to Area 11. You will meet her at Guinness City Centre. She's their Coordinator," she explained in a soft low voice.

Solomon was grateful as he took a cab to Guinness City Centre. When they got at a building jam-packed with people, they pulled over.

"Is this the Guinness City Centre?" Solomon asked the driver.

"Sure, this is the place you want to be," the driver answered, "this is Guinness City Centre."

Solomon stepped out of the car and walked through the long narrow walkway. He was very careful not to step on anybody.

"Let me through. I need to be around you," the driver trudged behind him. He wouldn't allow anybody between them.

"Excuse me, please. Let me through," Solomon said to somebody in front of him.

"Hey! No cutting in line. Wait for your turn, friend! We're here first," somebody shouted.

"I don't know who you think you are buddy. But I've been waiting two hours to get to this point. If you think you people can just waltz yourself in here and push in front of everyone. You're crazy. This line starts at the edge," another person shouted.

"Hey! I didn't come for the ticket. I'm a corp member. Where is the office of the coordinator?" Solomon asked the last speaker.

"There!" A man said and pointed at the third door in first floor. Solomon pushed through all the way like he did when he was coming in . With his steel-brown eyes shining in a way that would help him scare people off his way, he went up through the way back to the edge of the stairwell so that he could get to the Coordinator's office. When he got to the front door, he tended not to be doomed trying to hide his plans from Mrs. Barbra which he felt was more important. The door was steel metal with small hole almost eighteen inches down from the top where she could see people from inside. Solomon knocked, and stepped back a little. Seconds later, the door was opened.

"Solomon!" She called, and stepped aside for the two men to go in. She could tell from Solomon's countenance that all was not well with him.

"Welcome!" she said to the other man whom she presumed must be a driver.

Solomon was surprised at how she welcomed him. They had never been friends. Even when Oluchi died, Mrs. Barbra did not show up at the funeral service. Solomon bore all the expenses. But it was told how she cried...and cried for many days and refused to be consoled.

"Solomon you look haggard, what happened?" She asked.

"It's about Oluchi."

"This conversation is over," she said feeling very irritated. That statement sounded like a careless word in her hearing. What is it you still want from Oluchi even after she has died? Why wont you allow her spirit to rest?

"Please madam, you have to listen to me. Oluchi was not buried properly. I need her to rest in peace."

When she heard that, Mrs. Barbra became more disturbed. She couldn't do nothing than to let tears gushed out from her eyes just like the day Oluchi was buried. The pains in her heart were like cancer pains; and it spread like bacteria slowly. She sat down on her swivel chair and bent her head. It was obvious she was terrified. Solomon himself didn't know the right thing to say or do, so he kept quiet. He doubted if she would want to hear the rest of the message that brought him to her office. Having cried enough, she stood up and gained bearing.

"All right. What about her?" She asked in a very firm voice.

"I need you to come with me to see a man of God who conducted a deliverance on Oluchi. This man here is a driver I hired from Enugu so you won't bother with an extra expenses on trip back to this place; he has been paid for that."

"You want me to follow you to Enugu?" Mrs Barbra asked in a

voice that gave Solomon an inkling that she knew exactly what she was needed for. But Mrs. Barbra had learnt from her previous attempts to rescue Oluchi, not to be fastidious in anything that had to do with Oluchi. She watched her husband die for the same course. She had mellowed down, after her madness, in her search for Oluchi's deliverance. And now that Oluchi has gone, she wouldn't want to have anything more to do with her.

"Are you under a curse?" she asked Solomon.

Solomon looked at her. All the while, he was worried about the way she was looking at him. It was there in the movement of those deep eyes that were constantly staring at him.

"I appreciate your concern madam. Please I wish we leave in the morning to be there in time," Solomon pleaded. Mrs. Barbra sat down again disheartened, disillusioned, tears were running down her eyes; and the wall clock struck three o'clock.

NINE

Emmanuel came back, dropped his small brown bag on the table, and lay in his bed. He was so tired that he couldn't remove his shoes. After resting for few minutes, he remembered that he had an appointment with the lawyer he intended to use to follow up Peter's case so he stood up and left. Peter had been in police detention for some days now without any serious attention given to him. It was Adanna who gave him the address on how to contact the lawyer. When he got to the address, he met nobody. He was told that the lawyer had gone out two days earlier and would return the next day. So he left.

Emmanuel had been so worried lately. He was worried about Peter's fate and that of Adanna. He had realised how deeply he loved Adanna these few days she had been indisposed. He then told himself that he had been interested in Adanna long before now. It was during their little affair that Adanna fell ill. She had been in the hospital for five days even though the doctor had assured him that she would be okay.

Emmanuel was undecided whether to go home and rest , to go and visit Adanna in the hospital or to go and see Peter.

"I have to go and see Peter," he resolved. So he walked some metres away from the lawyer's house and flagged down a taxi to the mechanic workshop where he picked up his car.

When he got to the police station, there were only two cars at the parking lobby so he comfortably parked his own. He stared at the building for some minutes, stepped out of the car and walked into the building.

After about seven minutes of delay, Peter was brought out by a fierce looking police officer with his hands behind-, handcuffed. Emmanuel and Peter sat opposite each other and discussed. That was not Peter's first time of being arrested by the police. He had had experiences, but that day, he said to Emmanuel in tears and pains;

"This place is not a hotel room. Please get me out of here." Emmanuel sat there staring into space.

"For three days now, this is my first time of sitting down. Look at my legs," he said and raised his legs for Emmanuel to see.

"I do not eat. I'm just given only water. We are twenty- seven inmates in my cell room," he paused. Then he continued; "there's just no space to rest or sit down. Just yesterday, two inmates died of suffocation."

Emmanuel felt for him. He wouldn't want to start regretting getting Peter involved in Oluchi's case. The deed has been done. There's no point crying over spilt milk.

"All right," Emmanuel said, "I am working with Human Rights to get you out of here. Probably, you will come out tomorrow."

"Ok, that's good. Please you'll need to be fast in whatever you're doing. It seems they want to take my case to Federal Detention."

"Federal Detention!" That sounded as a warning to Emmanuel. It was not going to be easy there. He had nothing to say to Peter again so he stood up and left. There were fewer people outside unlike when he came in. Most people were heading through a long narrow walkway to the main gate. Emmanuel walked through the walkway. Just before a step out of the building, fingers rested on his shoulder so he turned to see who the owner of the fingers was. To his greatest surprise, it was Victoria! She was the last person he ever wanted to bump into. At that moment, he rued visiting Peter. He stood in surprise as he looked at her. It took him more than twenty-five seconds to steady his breath.

"What are you doing here?" He asked in wonderment.

Victoria grinned. "I work with the police. I'm a Federal agent, Intelligence Department." She explained, smiling.

"So, what brought you here?" She asked him.

Emmanuel said nothing but continued staring at her in surprise. Victoria smiled again. The same smile she used the day she lured him into having sex with her. An act he would continue to regret all the days of his life. He remembered the night again. The night she had quoted for him the full meaning of betrayal. Emmanuel sighed and said, "A friend of mine was arrested over a stolen car. But today, they changed his case file to trespass."

"What's his name and who is his I.O?" She asked him. Emmanuel told her as two of them walked to the main gate. She told him the importance of getting a lawyer before she left.

Emmanuel sat in his car and thought things over; and then he decided to try another lawyer before going home that day. Peter need to regain his freedom. He reasoned, bitterly.

* * *   * * *

When Solomon and Mrs. Barbra got Enugu, it was no longer raining. But the weather was still very cold. Solomon intently stared at Mrs. Barbra. He was worried that the man of God might say something they could not handle. Emmanuel moved closer to Solomon, "The doctor said Adanna could be in trouble," he said to Solomon in a low tone.

"What does he mean by being in trouble? Is Adanna seriously ill?" Solomon asked.

"He said it's HPV … 'Human Papilloma Virus," Emmanuel replied.

"Meaning?" Solomon asked looking worried.

"He said that cervical cancer could be within reach in her case; her skin is changing."

"That's all right. Please let's suspend this conversation for the mean time. We will discuss it later," Solomon pleaded. There was a tone of finality in his voice. He was really feeling the weight of the world on his little shoulders. Though he felt terrible to hear that Adanna was seriously ill yet the emergency of dealing with the issue of Oluchi and her mother would not allow him to visit her. He had not forgotten his appointment with the man of God so he needed to employ an idea for that since he could not hide things from him. He bore no grudge against anybody. His only regret in life was the day he met Oluchi.

"If Oluchi was to return to this world, I would still marry her?" Solomon said. In his mind, he was just a blind man doing his time in Oluchi's penitentiary. Mrs. Barbra tried imagining what addiction could cause in a man's life, then what anybody's dependency could mean to him or her. She was right that Solomon had lost his sense of reasoning. This wasn't about people making friends, but about friends meeting friends. Since she had moved on with her life after the madness, she felt as though nothing in her life was her own. Mrs. Barbra confirmed that the medicine man was right about what he had said in prophecy. Really, things have escalated much more.

"You will not marry her young man," Mrs. Barbra said. She was still prepared to say more things regardless of what had happened. She felt bad that Solomon disrespected her, got her annoyed and that was more than anything she could take. She needed to convince him that he was doing a wrong thing. She adjusted in her chair. In her mind, it was the only right thing to do in order to keep Solomon alive, so she did not feel guilty about what she was about doing.

"You don't know Oluchi, do you?" She asked him.

Solomon would have said yes, but he needed to hear more from her because the man of God told him he was no longer what he seemed to be. He would find answers to that too.

The time was 11:09am. Without saying a word, Mrs. Barbra stormed out of the room. She gave Solomon a look that was mixed with anger and disappointment. She looked at her wristwatch perhaps to guess how long it would take her to explain things to Solomon and make him reconsider that he's going to be no more. Solomon had made the same major mistake young men make at times without considering its consequences. Yes, he was right about love, yet he was wrong about customs and traditions. But if Mrs. Barbra had to say to Solomon that Oluchi's life was prophesied, once this fact has been established to his understanding, Solomon would not have time to live but to join Oluchi. That was the message. It was said that the ear that hears it will go deaf. It was a difficult request to grant. But Mrs. Barbra said, "I will tell you."

She then adjusted her chair and stared at Solomon for some minutes. Then she began:

"The land of Umualamaeze was once filled with righteous men and noble men. But later, only murderers remained. The people of our land were no longer progressing. Young ladies suffered the pains of spinsterhood, and women became childless. The gods were angry. It was not a village where you should marry from. The life you are living today is useless. It cannot be redeemed. Oluchi's birth was prophesied. It was told before the day I conceived her that she would destroy as many lives as possible. There was no redemption for people who slept with her."

When Solomon heard that, he mumbled, "The same day, I will collapse like a king, a new king, who will be free from this bondage, will arise. I will write a book to teach the youth about sex and relationship. Sex is not romantic." He reasoned.

His mind was not with Mrs. Barbra when she called his attention. The time was passing by and they needed to see the man of God. Solomon watched as Emmanuel and Mrs. Barbra left the room and as the door closed. He realized Mrs. Barbra was right about sleeping with Oluchi. Sex was the total commitment he ever did. It was just an emotional and spiritual covenant of blood for blood. Making friends was all about context, but sex was another thing which changed the direction of his affairs, destiny and fate. Solomon felt before people would pull off their clothes, there were things they may need to know.

When Solomon was in his early twenties, he was in love with Victoria and he never knew he was going to leave her for the sake of what she did. If pains were romance, then Victoria was very romantic. He thought he was going to continue loving her even when she was not emotionally sorry for sleeping with Emmanuel. He was still nursing the open wounds Victoria gave him when he met Oluchi, so he fell madly in love with her.

Solomon sighed, stood up and went to join Emmanuel and Mrs. Barbra in the car. When they got to the ministry, Solomon's eyes never left Mrs Barbra as they went in one after another. They took the second entrance to the sitting-room and sat down. They heard faint footsteps approaching and knew that man of God had come. The man of God stood at the door for a while and said some prayers. Afterwards, he entered the room and greeted all of them

"You're welcome in Jesus' name."

Solomon could sense fear all around him. The more he tried to push it off, the more it enveloped him. He closed his eyes, took a long deep breath. When he opened his eyes, the wall clock struck 3o' clock .He became more convinced than ever that he was in deep trouble. Then he said to himself, "Of course, I can ask God for forgiveness and beg Him to redeem my life. I'm only a human being, I have been made to understand that sleeping with any woman could change my fate and yet, bring death." That time, the message came to him that something was really wrong with him indeed. He cleared his throat and waited no more as he proceeded to talk to the man of God.

"Can one night take away the breath of life the Lord has given to me? Can't this prophecy be opposed?"he asked the man of God.

The man of God shook his head and said, "This is an alert from the river goddess and so let no one worry about it, for the Lord is good." Always let dreams alarm you. I wish to return your bad dreams and its explanations back to your enemies, not to you. Always let God who leads you- guide you," he repeated.

"All that happened to you was to tell you who you are," Mrs. Barbra said. "only six days later, after you finished working out for Oluchi's deliverance that you messed up your life. Look at how great your life was before you met Oluchi. Don't it bother you?"

Solomon was about to talk when a voice spoke; "Solomon listen to what they are saying, when your sanity returns, when your honour returns, then you will sing praises to God." It was Emmanuel who said it.

After that, Mrs. Barbra continued;

"Many years ago, during the enthronement of King Geoffrey George, the king of Umualamaeze village, and my husband was the kingmaker of the land of Umualamaeze. On that night, they were to make a sacrifice with a virgin girl, so they killed a six-year old girl named Anuli and offered her as a sacrifice. Anuli was the only daughter of one mad woman in the neighbouring village. After that, King Geoffrey invited his cabinet members to a great feast, and they drank wine together. While they were still drinking, my husband, Christopher, gave an order to bring in the golden and silvery cups, and bowls which his father had carried from the shrine. Immediately those items were brought in, the cabinet members started singing some songs, thanking the god of gold, silver, bronze, iron, wood, and stone. Suddenly the gods became angry, and a hand appeared and began to write on the plaster wall of the shrine where the light from the lamps was shining most brightly. King Geoffrey saw the writings, and turned pale. He was so frightened that his knees began to shake. He shouted for somebody to bring Christopher. When Christopher came, the king pleaded to him that someone should read the writing and tell him what it means; that If anyone does it, the person would be dressed in robes of royal purple, wear golden chains of honour round his neck and he would be the third in power of this kingdom.' That night, all the royal advisers came , but none of them was able to interpret the message. The king sent for all the male children to come to the shrine. It was a fearful day. The queen mother heard the noise made by the king and his noblemen so she sent a message to the king about a great medicine man in the neighbouring village. She wrote to the king saying, "When your father was the king, there was a man who showed some good sense, knowledge, and wisdom; like wisdom of the gods. And your father made him the chief of the fortune-tellers, magicians, wizards. He has an unusual ability, and he is wise and skillful in interpreting dreams, solving riddles, and explaining mysteries. So, send for this man, Richard, whom the king- your father named 'half spirit, half human, a burning flame' and he will tell you the meaning of the writings on the wall. The king gave an order and few minutes later, Richard was brought before the king. 'Are you Richard, whom my father said was from the spirit-world?' The king asked and the man nodded. The king continued,' None of my people was able to interpret this writing on the wall and tell me the meaning. I heard that you can find hidden knowledge and explain mysteries. If you can read this writing and tell me what it means, you will be dressed in robes of royal purple and a gold chain of honour round your neck, and would be the third in power of this great kingdom.'

To everybody's surprise, Mrs Barbra continued, "the man said to the king, 'Keep your gifts to yourself, or give them to someone else. I will read for Your Majesty what has been written and tell you the meaning. 'The gods of our land made your father a great king and gave him dignity and majesty. He was so great that people of other kingdoms, races, and languages were afraid of him and his kingdom. They trembled at mention of his name. He became so proud, stubborn, and cruel. Consequently, he was removed from his royal throne and lost his place of honour. He was killed by the god of our land which is the god of the river. And you, his son succeeded him by human society and cultural heritage. Because you have no guide from the gods, you have not humbled yourself before the gods of our land, even though you knew all these. You acted against the gods of the land. You took cups and bowls from the shrine. You, your cabinet members and your wives drank from them and praised the gods made of gold, silver, bronze, iron, wood, and stone. The god of the river is a jealous god. You did not honour her who determines if you live or die. That is why the gods have sent the hand to write this message. This is what was written: **'Number, number, weight, and division'** and this is what it means, **Number:** the gods have numbered your days. **Number:** the gods have numbered the days of your kingdom and brought it to an end. **Weight:** you have been weighed on a scale and found to be too light. **Division:** your kingdom is divided. Immediately King Geoffrey George ordered his servants to dress Richard in robes of royal purple and to put a gold chain of honour round his neck. And he made him the third in power in the kingdom.

That same night, King Geoffrey Gorge was visited by the river goddess, and he did not see the next day. Christopher my husband was then forty-two years old. He seized the royal power. The river goddess denied us children. When we went to her to plead for forgiveness, she told us that my husband and the cabinet members killed a child she projected into the world with a great mission. She said many things and told us that we would beget a child. That her name would be Oluchi and she would be the destroyer of the kingdom, after which she would raise a king in Umualamaeze village. To the goddess, Oluchi, meant a human spiritual tool. No one who slept with her was meant to stay alive. She told my husband that he would sleep with her for three times on three different market days, "Mrs. Barbra narrated in tears. If she could, she would continue, but tears had covered her eyes. Her mouth and her tongue were vibrating.

"You were not meant to marry her. She was not meant to be married," she finally said with her head bent.

Solomon did not ask why again for he heard all she said. He felt he deserved pity because he had made a mistake that was common to most young men.

With four of them in the apartment, the pastor felt he had not seen anything like that in his life. All Solomon wanted was the chance of a fresh start ,would that be given to him? Nobody knows. The woman he felt comfortable with had a spiritual problem. She was a steady threat to his life and he didn't notice it. What kept him going was the hope he got as a Christian. When the pastor said something that bothered him, he didn't do a thing. He felt that he had time to perfectly choose the pathway for his life. The amount of prayers needed to redeem his life was another thing that bothered his thinking system at every second.

"DO YOU UNDERSTAND? Your life is in real trouble," the pastor said to Solomon.

* * * * * *

Adanna lay in the hospital bed which was covered with white bedspread, a drip-stand was by her side. Her eyes were closed. Emmanuel was walking up and down in the room. He was deeply worried about the virus that was eating away Adanna's life. He felt he could do something but he didn't know what exactly. The doctor

100

had assured him the previous night that all would be well if only there would be money to perform the surgery before it would develop a cervical cancer.

"Why does it have to be me?" Emmanuel asked himself as he walked to the window with his hands across his chest. He peered through the window. Looking at his poise which was casual and satisfying you would think that all's well. Something he learnt from his father.

"I have just few friends in this world, yet they die one after another. Perhaps, because of something we did earlier in life," he mumbled. Then the doctor walked into the room carrying some medical reports in his hand.

"Who will sign for her?" The doctor asked Emmanuel.

"I will do that sir," Emmanuel said.

"Follow me then," the doctor said and left the room. Emmanuel turned and looked at Adanna who was lying helplessly in the bed and wished she could just open her eyes and looked at him. He knew he might not be the right person to sign on any authorization paper, but he was the person that brought her to the hospital. Without looking for the parents, he had signed the admission papers. He was truly racking with his brain as he climbed the stairwell that led to the doctor's office. On getting to the doctor's office, he knocked and went in.

"Sit down Mr. Emmanuel," the doctor said to Emmanuel.

"Nice office you've got here. Could you please reduce the air-conditioner?" Emmanuel requested. He was feeling very cold having been indoors with Adanna all day.

"Of course yes."

Taking Adanna to the hospital for days had given Emmanuel the responsibility he never envisaged in his life. He continued looking intently at the doctor as the doctor assembled some papers from the big folder in front of him..While waiting for the doctor, Emmanuel remembered the first time he met Adanna. She was looking very healthy and beautiful. But now who could believed that she was the same Adanna who was lying unconsciously in the hospital bed with her life ebbing away as each second passed. But isn't that what life is all about- blossoming today and withering tomorrow? Emmanuel raged.

Few minutes later, the doctor adjusted himself in his chair. Emmanuel's face became thinner as if the bones underneath were pushing themselves outward to show how fearful he was. His countenance betrayed his confidence.

"Mr. Emmanuel?" The doctor called.

"There is something I would like you to know," he said with some amount of seriousness.

Emmanuel's heart skipped again when he heard that. But he encouraged himself that he wouldn't flinch in doing anything that would make Adanna to regain her health and be well again.

"This is a case of Human Papilloma Virus (HPV). HPV is an infection contracted through sexual related activities. It is dangerous and kills slowly," the doctor explained painstakingly. He then gave Emmanuel a pen to put down anything he didn't understand. Emmanuel collected the pen from him with shaky hands.

"This disease has progressed to precancerous lesions and invasive cancer of the cervix would be next. Ninety percent of this disease is gone in two years. And the process usually takes ten to fifteen years. Provided there are early opportunities of detection and treatment of the precancerous lesion, but progression to invasive cancer can be prevented when standard prevention strategies are employed," the doctor said, paused for some seconds and continued, "the disease cause considerable burden necessitating preventive surgeries which do, in many cases involve loss of fertility. One more thing. We used liquid-based cytology to detect that your friend has adenocarcinoma ... and over 3000 people died in U S. in 2008 because of cancer of the cervix."

Emmanuel dropped his pen and asked, "What is ADENOCARCINOMA?"

"It is a vaginal glandular tumor," the doctor explained. When he saw how frightful Emmanuel was looking, he said, "I am not saying that your friend will die. The chances of survival are just less than 50%, and the chances of loss of fertility are less than 30%. I'm just telling you all these things so that you will know why you should or should not sign those papers," he explained, pointing at the papers.

Emmanuel sat, shaking his two legs. He was anxious about the difficult decision he was about to make. The only person who would understand his dilemma was Solomon. Over the last few seconds that went by, all he was thinking was what would happen if something went wrong. Truly, it was a difficult decision to take. Now he could not concentrate to make up his mind on supporting the doctor to go ahead with the surgery. No matter what might be the case, he was the one that brought her to this hospital and since then Adanna had not even opened her eyes even to say thank you talk more of eliciting any information about her family from her. Emmanuel remembered that he promised to take care of her even at the point of death. Solomon had also told him that if he were to be burdened with Adanna's case that he would go to St. John's Parish and do his first thanksgiving.

Our God is a merciful one. He made us and brought us where we are. He still cares for us, Emmanuel reasoned. He brought out his hand-phone from his pocket, dialed Solomon's phone-number and waited for a response. If at the end of the ring Solomon did not pick up the call, would he sign it? At that time, a male voice sounded in response.

"Hello!"

"Good!" Emmanuel felt relieved.

"This is Emmanuel Ibe; I'm calling from Precious Specialist Hospital."

The receiver interrupted him. "Emmanuel, I know. It's me Solomon, what's up?" The voice sounded so coarse that Emmanuel wondered if he was really speaking with Solomon or a fraudster.

"Solomon, I'm in the hospital where Adanna is on admission. There are some decisions to take here and I need a witness; so I was thinking if you could just come over. My hands are too tight."

"How is Adanna?" Solomon asked. That question made Emmanuel remember when Esther passed away and Oluchi called Solomon to come over to the hospital.

"She's going to undergo a surgery in few hours from now. The doctor needs me to sign some documents and you to second me."

"Okay!" Solomon said and shrugged at the change of plans. He had wanted to go and get the dress Mrs. Barbra wore all the years of her madness.

"I will be there in few minutes," he finally said over the phone.

"Thanks."

* * *   * * *

After taking his bath, he came out from the bathroom and slipped into his pyjamas. The pyjamas was very fanciful with red-edged, white silk with his initials on the jacket pocket. He sat on the edge of the bed, said his prayers and lay down, facing the ceiling.

It was nearly four and half an hour past the normal time he usually went to bed yet sleep eluded him. He tossed and turned in the bed. His heart was very heavy.

"My life was going to settle down into a happy groove. My writing career was going well. God! The money I got from stories averaged forty thousand naira a month, and with my work as a corp member which brought me to about nineteen thousand, eight hundred naira to add to myself. And if work had sparked and Oluchi didn't come, I could have started writing my second novel. Emmanuel is on a new book too; and we spent most of our time together learning how to write movies and become movie directors. Now, I have ended up everything I worked for. I didn't think anything would happen. But, was it true that Oluchi had covered my eyes and I chose to call it love. That relationship was improper," Solomon lamented aloud, "look at me, a grandson of Chief Edie Okafor. A self-made graphic designer, a budding novelist. I know I was the best of my kind. Who is going to talk about colour separations without contacting me? I was going to be interviewed by Nigerian Writers' Forum for being the writer of the biggest volume novel of the year. I spent sleepless nights writing that book: "Gone To Island" Now, what will happen to all the benefits? Wow! I'm screwed." Tears rained down his face; he did not stop them rather he leaned forward and held his pillow very tightly as if he was dragging it with somebody. He could not explain it. With the heaviness in his heart, he did not know when he slept off. At midnight, Solomon began talking even he was the only person in the whole house. His body began shaking vigourously. Suddenly, he stopped talking and fell into deep sleep.

Solomon saw himself stood before a large mirror. He was about going out but he was not satisfied on the attire he was putting on. He wondered if he had chosen the best attire. He wore a purple long-sleeved shirt on blue jeans. He wiped off the sweat on his brow, took a deep breath, opened the front door and left. As he was climbing down the stairs, he saw a familiar face coming towards him. He knew that face- a grinning beautiful Oluchi again! She stood on the doorstep, dressed in a linen jacket and jeans, holding a bottle of

Amarula medium bottle-wine. She looked prettier than ever. She had done something different to her hair. Solomon had never seen this set of clothes she wore; and her skin was glowing.

"I think I left you for so long?" She apologised, smiling.

"This is for you; your last fantasy," she said as she handed the bottle of wine to Solomon.

"Cheers. Thanks for the wine, That was really very kind of you" Solomon said and pecked her. And both of them walked back inside the house, and then inside the bedroom.

"How have you been managing since I left?" She asked him, as she undid her jacket. Solomon ogled at her and admired her dress. Under the jacket, she wore a red-patterned top that showed her bare shoulders.

"Fine, not really fine," Solomon replied.

"Nice top," he finally said.

"Ha -ha -ha … don't worry my love," she said and held his hand, "This is where the journey ends. I'm going to take you with me and everything will be fine," she said assuredly leading him out of the bedroom.

With their hands together, they made their way to the exit door, then out of the building. Solomon was oblivious of where he was being taken to. They took each other's arm as they walked down an unfamiliar avenue. The big trees by the two sides of the street were old, the walkway was lonely, the long street was empty yet they continued walking. They got to a junction and branched to the left. After the junction was a small stream that led to a bigger one, then to a river where many people were not particularly concerned to swim. But people passed by. She took the drink she had come with, opened the bottle and with her right hand raised in toast, and said;

"Your life will pass away like the flower of a wild plant. When the sun rises with its blazing heat and burns the plant; its flowers fall off, and its beauty is destroyed. That same way your life has gone with me!"

Solomon smiled. Really, he had nothing to say, He did not notice anything. It was just like fanning flame. As if he was blind to the fact that real thing was happening because he had no God. They continued. They were just no more, no less than good lovers. It was a real party going on. Afterwards, Oluchi talked Solomon into swimming in the river and he agreed; even though they had some good drink. They had only been in the water ten minutes when Emmanuel from nowhere noticed that Solomon was missing. Oluchi was laughing with her two hands up. She was looking at the sky as if she was talking or laughing with somebody upwards.

"The world will grow dim."

Emmanuel searched the river to see Solomon but it was too late. Solomon's body was found six hours later. It was terrible. It was the worst thing Solomon had ever experienced. Even till then, it didn't seem real because Solomon was the one experiencing this. For minutes, he tried to make sense out of it but he could not. It just seemed so senseless. Such a waste!

Solomon woke up with a start. But he could not explain, neither could he understand what happened. It seemed that it was the end of his life and the end of life itself

* * *   * * *.

Dawn has come and everybody had gone out for business. It wasn't too early for Mrs. Barbra's calls. She was supposed to call Solomon to pick her up, but she hadn't called. So, Solomon bought some magazines and read them, then he had coffee and a sandwich. When he heard an announcement on the television that a long bus coming to Enugu had an accident earlier that morning, he went downstairs, locked up his doors and hurried to the park where he had waited for her the previous day. As usually with transport business, everybody was on his own. By the time most of the passengers were milling around the place where their luggage was kept, Solomon still could not see Mrs. Barbra. He kept looking for her. Everybody that boarded last night including some of the people who boarded the bus involved in the accident were coming out except for those who died at the spot and had been taken to the hospital for confirmation. The crowd began to thin out and after a while, there were only few suitcases left.

Solomon called the pastor and asked him if there were any call from Mrs. Barbra and the pastor said no. Then Solomon called Guinness City Centre and asked if Mrs. Barbra was in his office. They told him that she had traveled to Enugu on a night bus. He became confused. He picked up the phone again and called M700 Transport Information Agency and asked them if Mrs. Barbra Egwuatu had been in the bus that had accident. They answered in positive. Solomon was overwhelmed with fear. Then the man continued.

"Yes, she made a reservation, but did not show up," the man finally said.

Solomon became worried but he figured something out. Mrs. Barbra had told the driver that brought them down to Enugu the first time that she might call him to come and pick her. Some last minutes emergency had made Solomon change course because he was sure that she would get in touch with him if something arose, that she would never hang up. She had always told him of any change of plans, and that, in her own way she was too considerate to let him go to the park and wait for hours when she knew she wouldn't be coming. And yet it took Solomon almost the whole day not hearing from her and not being able to figure out where she was before Solomon called Emmanuel.

Emmanuel was glad to hear from Solomon at that point in time.

His voice sounded very strong and very healthy unlike when he had called him for Adanna. Solomon told him that Mrs. Barbra was missing. Solomon told him that her line wasn't going and that he had checked out for her at Guinness City Centre, M700 Transport Information Agency and even the hotel where she slept the last time she came to Enugu.

"Why don't you be my guest right now. The pastor has promised to put your mind to rest," was all Emmanuel could say.

"Emmanuel, what's going on? Have you heard from Mrs. Barbra?" Solomon wondered.

"Why don't you come over?"

All right, I will soon join you," he finally said and breathed a sigh of relief. He was sure that if he meet Mrs. Barbra, that everything would be all right with him again. As he had thought early in the morning before he became worried that she might have been involved in the accident. Had it been that really Mrs Barbra was involved in any accident, that would have been his end.

Then the moment Solomon got to the pastor's house and saw Mrs. Barbra. His head began to swell. A part of him left him. There was something about the dress Mrs. Barbra's was wearing especially her blouse . But in keeping faith with what the pastor told him the previous day, there was hope for him. Solomon tried to recover his composure immediately. With a beaming smile, Solomon held the pastor's hand.

"Good afternoon pastor."

"Please sit down," the pastor responded.

He greeted Mrs. Barbra and Emmanuel. Emmanuel stared at him and wondered why Solomon reacted the way he did when he walked into the room. Solomon could not take her eyes off Mrs Barbra's blouse.

A scientific examination into Solomon's head at that moment, would have revealed a total brainstorm. He was convinced he could neither see nor hear, and that his vision was already blurred. His stomach turned and rumbled that he felt an overwhelming urge to take a trip to the loo. His knees were wobbling as he embarked on the trip.

"Oluchi and her mother..... the same dress" his mind was chanting continuously as if he took some mescaline. The voices continued chanting, "Should I run away? Should I run away? Should I runaway?" in his head. Seconds later, the words changed and he began to hear, "I am going to die, I am going to die, I am going to die"

As the panic and the voices subsided a little, Solomon came out from the loo and joined others. The six eyes were on him.

"Ehe...m pastor," Solomon said, and cleared his throat, "shall we begin?"

"What's up man? You look a shadow of yourself." Emmanuel asked him. Solomon didn't say a word to Emmanuel rather he turned to Mrs. Barbra and said;

"I hope you wouldn't mind showing us the clothes now?

Mrs. Barbra kept quiet. Emmanuel became more confused.

"I had a horrible dream last night. That dream tolled the death knell for a new life for me outside here. Time is ticking away."Solomon said

"Where is your faith brother?" The pastor queried.

"Well, pastor, the problem is ... There is something you haven't quite ... understood," Solomon said, picking his words, "it's like this .... There's a little bit of problem with this woman."He said, pointing at Mrs. Barbra. Emmanuel and the pastor were surprised, but Mrs Barbra was not ,rather she kept nodding her head.

"Solomon, what is it?" Emmanuel asked.

"Well, the problem is ... This woman is not exactly .... I don't know how to put it...," Solomon said trying to explain.

"Just come out with it," Emmanuel pleaded. He was becoming afraid.

"Well, pastor," Solomon began, " do you know this woman sitting in this room with us?"

The pastor and Emmanuel turned to see if there was another woman in the room except Mrs Barbra.

"This woman came to my dream last night and killed me.. It was Emmanuel who rescued my dead body after about six hours of search in a river. I died last night. She was wearing this same dress, no, this same top," he explained.

Everybody was surprised and speechless except Mrs. Barbra who stood up.

"Pastor this is the dress. I would like to take my leave now," she said, handed the pastor a small polythene bag and left.

That explained many things to all of them; why her sentence constructions went all weird whenever she spoke about her daughter Oluchi, but none of them considered it a big deal. The pastor quicky opened the bag that was given to him and in the bag was the same dress, same top she was wearing before she left.

KINGDOM FAR AWAY

It was six thirty on a Friday night, two days after his deliverance. Solomon was sitting in front of the TV waiting for Emmanuel and Adanna to get back from the hospital. Since he had finished for the day an hour earlier, he had put the dish washer on, tidied the kitchen after cooking dinner. He prepared the remaining ingredients for storage.

He had just finished watching Super Story and was about watching the seven o' clock news when he heard the sound of Emmanuel's Mercedes Benz outside.

He opened the door and welcomed them. Emmanuel moved in first while Adanna followed him behind. Solomon planted a warm kiss on her right cheek and she smiled. He apologised to Adanna for his inability to accompany Emmanuel to the hospital to bring her home.

"You're welcome my love. I have prepared your favourite dinner this evening, just for you and you alone," Solomon said grinning.

Adanna beamed with delight when she heard that.

"It's good to hear that," she said weakly.

"I must tell you, you are looking good now," Solomon complemented her.

"The doctor said so. But I don't think I'm ok because my head is still too heavy for me to carry, Adanna said. The two men's eyes met and they burst into laughter. Solomon stopped laughing as he remembered what was said about his own life.

Emmanuel watched as Adanna walked unsteadily to the chair and sat down. She was looking taller, slimmer, calmer and more graceful. She was not what he would call beautiful with her thick lips, brown bulging eyes and small nose, yet, all these were what sent a hot wave of blood running through Emmanuel each time he looked at her. Emmanuel came closer and saw that her knees were pressed together and her two hands were resting on a black leather handbag. He had sworn eternal friendship with her because of his deep affection for her. He took off her shoes from her feet, collected her bag from and dropped them on the floor. His eyes caught her long fingers and well manicured nails and they appealed to his senses. He imagined the erotic feelings he would get if those fingers were to start working on his body.

"Take my handbag," Adanna said to Emmanuel, "there's three thousand naira in there with drugs. The doctor said he had the drugs specified," she explained. Emmanuel pulled her gently toward him.

Solomon sat there watching as Emmanuel took her by the arm and led her to the next room. He had begged them to come over and stay with him because he was scared of sleeping alone at night. Twenty minutes later, they had finished having their bath so Solomon served the dinner. They all relished the perfect culinary skill Solomon exhibited in preparing rice

After the meal, the trio were in high spirit as they discussed and laughed boisterously. Emmanuel became more in love and attracted to Adanna that at the time both of them forgot that Solomon was still there with them and talked about only the things that concerned both of them. Solomon smiled at the two love birds and kept himself busy with the television. Emmanuel's only worry then was how long it would take before Adanna recovered very well so that he could show her how deeply he had fallen in love with her. When Adanna started yawning, Emmanuel helped her into the room and made her lay comfortably in the bed. When he was sure she was okay, he knelt by her side and said few words of prayer for her asking God to forgive them their sins and give Adanna a total healing and quick recovery.

Solomon's eyes followed them to the bedroom. He was greatly pleased. He reached for the pack of cracker biscuits that was on the centre table in the sitting room and took some. Emmanuel came out and joined him and they munched in silence. The fact that his life had just been dissolved weakened him. But he felt strengthened that Adanna and Emmanuel had redeemed theirs and would make a perfect match.

Solomon yawned and stood up from the chair. Without saying a word to Emmanuel, he started going to his bedroom. Emmanuel went after him.

"Solomon, why do you listen to people who say your life cannot be redeemed? You can see for yourself that the Lord we serve is the

Lord of host. Adanna's life had just been redeemed. So, why will you lose faith and say that the deliverance will not work?"

The remaining biscuit Solomon had in his hand fell to the floor, and scattered into pieces. He turned his face away and said; "*The year Uzziah died, Isaiah saw the Lord.*" Then he began to weep. The statement terrified Emmanuel. As he stood there gaping, Solomon went into his room and lay down. Emmanuel reluctantly rejoined Adanna who was already fast asleep.

* * *   * * *

Two days later, on the twelfth day after the death of Oluchi. Solomon and Emmanuel arrived from the church after the deliverance. They had burnt the clothes Mrs. Barbra wore during her days of madness, made some prayers, and sacrifices. The pastor told Solomon that the spirit has gone never to return again, and that he should agree with him that his life had been redeemed. Solomon believed him. When they got home, they discovered that Solomon's pictures had been burnt too; leaving only the part where he appeared alone. Likewise, he found out that some of his properties were missing, as he tried to rearrange his house. Emmanuel went to the sitting room and replaced part of the things he had gathered from the kitchen which was formally placed in the sitting room.

"It's all over." This was the only thing that came from Solomon's lips.

That night when everybody had gone to sleep, Solomon stayed awake saying prayers to the Lord who had been good to him. After praying for ten minutes, he stopped. He put on his night wear and relaxed in the bed. His thought flashed back to the story of his life which he would gladly tell the whole world. The urge to put in black and white his next story based on the things that happened to him was very strong But what will be the title of my story?" He asked himself.

Maybe,

"The Story of my Life," or

"Is there another kingdom far away?" He grinned.

"Though I may not know the title now but I must write to the world," he thought again.

"The story I will write will be humourous and intriguing. It will be so unlike any of the things that happen in this world. But, my novel will not be jejune. My novel will keep my readers glued to it from start to finish. The world has got to be addressed to steer clear of premarital sex," Solomon said and smiled.

Solomon was a writer. A very good historical novelist. So he was sure that his next novel would be a classic one and would top the list in Amazon! Solomon's thought shifted to Emmanuel and Adanna. He tried not to think about Oluchi. Then he remembered Peter and wondered what he would be doing at that particular time. He lay propped against the pillows. He was going to reach out for his golden case of cigarette when his phone started ringing. He picked the phone and was astonished to hear Peter's voice. Why would Peter call him at that time of the day? He wondered. Peter had never called him before.

"Hello, Peter. I was just thinking about you. How are you?" Solomon said.

"That's just why I'm calling," he said, "you know I hurt my shoulder in the cell room. The doctor said I would be all right after one week."

"I'm so sorry to hear that. I had a couple of things in my hands lately but everything had been taken care of. The raised dust had settled," Solomon said with confidence.

"That's okay. I just called to know how you guys are doing. We'll see in the week."

"OK, good night."

155

It was late at night. Solomon brought out his writing materials and began to write. He wrote most of the night. It was at exactly two minutes past five in the morning that sleep conquered him and Solomon became his prisoner.

***** ***** *****

At 8:18am, Solomon was still sleeping even though the alarm clock had beeped as usual. He was obviously tired. Nobody bothered him. Adanna was sick. She was still sleeping even after Emmanuel had woken up. He quietly closed the door behind him leaving her alone with her weak system and restless heart. Adanna knew Emmanuel was up but she couldn't speak. Tears were rolling down her eyes. She was emotionally disturbed. Her head was still aching. She opened her mouth to call Emmanuel back but she decided against it. 'Sometimes in life, some stones are better left unturned. Whatever happened between Solomon and Oluchi was definitely one of those things. Oluchi ruined us.' She reasoned.

A sudden knock on the front door compelled Adanna to drag herself out of the bed. She wanted to know who the visitor was. When Emmanuel opened the door, the faces standing by the door looked familiar.

"My name is Robert Jerry. These men with me are my team members. Do you recognize me?

Emmanuel recognized him. He was a police officer. He once came to the house to speak with Oluchi over the case of a stolen car.

"Of course I do," Emmanuel said, shifting away from the door way. He halted when he saw Adanna standing behind him. She looked scared.

"What's going on?" She asked.

Emmanuel's attention shifted from Adanna to the police officers, from the officers back to Adanna. He leaned casually on the wall and said to Adanna;

"Please go and call Solomon for me. Tell him we have some visitors here." Adanna nodded and left.

Adanna entered the bedroom and called Solomon and he did not answer. As she stretched her right hand to wake him up, she saw something and took back her hand immediately. His pose was frightening. No one poised like that could sleep comfortably.

"Solomon!" She called again. Things really changed to her understanding. She stood transfixed on the ground. Then she remembered the curiosity in the policemen's eyes. Slowly, she moved closer and closer. Then, she had no real strength for all these.

"Solomon!!" She called the third time.

She studied the two innocent pillows by his side. The pillows were little far from each other. Adanna wanted to touch him. Just then, she saw his eyes- they were widely opened! She screamed, landed herself to the floor and remained there frozen. Emmanuel rushed in, the policemen followed him. Adanna was still there on the floor. Tears were gushing down from her eyes. She did not bother the tears. She allowed them.

Emmanuel took a very long deep breath when he saw Solomon's position. He was in the bed, lying cold. That was real thing. His throat became dried. All he kept saying in between tears was;

"It is not fair."

"It is never fair."

"This cannot be fair."

"This is so unfair."

The policemen were confused. They didn't know the next thing to do. They just stood there looking at Solomon unable to believe that he had just passed on.

In theory, it was just the prophecy, the great idea of Oluchi and her creator. To create from the created nature of human beings and bring them into their kingdom … it never stopped. They continued to make certain that all that slept with her and all that were willing to sleep with her were spiritually destroyed.

Though everybody was in the bedroom, there was a noise made through the kitchen. It wasn't a human being. It was Oluchi. She had just departed. She was there when everything was happening. It was her last resort.

That Tuesday evening, the policemen made call for an ambulance. Emmanuel and Adanna held each other. As long as Solomon lived, the kingdom of Oluchi would continue to oppress people through him. He died, for there to arise a king in the village of Umualamaeze.

Now the covenant Solomon made had been broken. The goddess of Umualamaeze village had found peace with her people again after so many years she abandoned them.

A will was established through a new born child.

I will never break my covenant with you. You must not make new covenant with people you meet on your way. Another hand wrote on the plastered wall of the shrine where the light from the lamp was shining most brightly.

The new child became the new king.

"Long live the king!

Let your will be done!

Let your kingdom come!" the people hailed.

***** ***** *****

Somewhere in a far away city, Emmanuel and Adanna were

living as husband and wife. They left after Solomon was buried to start afresh.

It was perhaps at the death of Solomon that people came to understand that sex as a covenant took Solomon out of the world. Solomon became ensnared and enslaved. He lived in bondage. He got himself into bondage with his promise. With advice of all kinds, he became a victim of incontinent bondage of life that had been kept running over the spiritual world.

KINGDOM FAR AWAY